THE VAMPIRE OF VOURLA

THE VAMPIRE OF VOURLA

and other Greek vampire tales, 1819-1846

Edited with an introduction by
Álvaro García Marín

VALANCOURT BOOKS

Published by Valancourt Books, Richmond, Virginia
http://www.valancourtbooks.com

ISBN 978-1-954321-75-5 (trade paperback)
Also available as an electronic book.

Cover by Xungarro   instagram.com/xungarro
Set in Dante MT

CONTENTS

INTRODUCTION

This book brings back to the reader a lost avenue of vampire fiction. Caught up in the standardized image cast by *Dracula* in 1897 and popularized by its cinematic sequels throughout the 20th and 21st centuries, we all "know" today the undead to be originally Romanian, or loosely Eastern European. However, that is not the whole picture. As late as 1929, Montague Summers wrote: "In no country has the vampire tradition more strongly prevailed and more persistently maintained its hold upon the people than in modern Greece."[1] And, in the same year, the American George Horton thought it fit to entitle his travel volume on the Greek islands *Home of Nymphs and Vampires.*[2]

This was not a coincidence. As I have shown elsewhere,[3] the first reports on vampirism to reach Western Europe during the 16th and 17th centuries came from modern Greece, then a part of the impenetrable Ottoman Empire. The enigmatic *vrykolakes* (singular *vrykolakas*), dead bodies thought by the Greeks to return from the grave to prey upon the living, were extensively discussed in learned circles—chiefly theological and antiquarian—for hundreds of years. So when in 1732, in a changing cultural context marked by incipient Enlightenment, news about massive vampire cases in Austrian-ruled Serbia burst into Western media, the European public used the Greek phenomenon as a yardstick to make sense of the

---

1 Montague Summers, *The Vampire in Europe* (New York: University Books, 1968 [1929]), 217.

2 George Horton, *Home of Nymphs and Vampires: The Isles of Greece* (Indianapolis: The Bobbs-Merrill Company, 1929).

3 Álvaro García Marín, "Haunted Communities: The Greek Vampire, or the Uncanny at the Core of Nation Formation," in *Monstrosity from the Inside Out*, edited by Teresa Cutler Broyles and Marko Theodorski (Oxford: Inter-Disciplinary Press, 2014), 109-142.

impressive accounts from the East. The newly introduced and quickly disseminated term "vampire" might well be Serbian or widely Slavic, but the ghastly tradition it described was originally from modern Greece. And, while the debate about chronological precedence of one regional form of vampirism over the others in Oriental Europe remains open even today—and is ultimately irrelevant—, these people got one thing right (perhaps the essential): the Serbian and the Greek monster, as well as their Polish, Romanian, or Russian counterparts, were basically one and the same creature—with minor variants.

It is thus only natural that by the turn of the 19th century, when the vampire—once the discussions on its scientific veracity were over—entered European literature as a mere fictional character, it did so in a predominantly Greek form and setting. In fact, it can be stated that the modern literary vampire emerged within the confines of two complementary discourses alternatively dominating Western culture in this period: classicist Hellenophilia and Romantic Philhellenism. This double allegiance attests on the one hand to the allegorical potential of the creature, suitable to address some of the pressing philosophical and political issues of the age (such as modernity's ambiguous relationship with Antiquity, cultural nostalgia, or anxiety over a rising historical consciousness founded upon a sense of break with the dead, irrecuperable past),[1] and, on the other, to the polysemy of Greekness, murkily split, like the vampire itself, between two temporally disconnected locations: the long departed Ancient Hellenic culture, and the contemporary territories of the Levant inhabited by Greek-speaking Orthodox Christians aiming for national independence.

The two first milestones of the genre, Goethe's *The Bride of Corinth* (1797) and Byron's *The Giaour* (1813), which paved the way for the modern vampire myth in both high and more

1 For this issue, see Claudia Lindén and Hans Ruin, "The Vampire, the Undead and the Anxieties of Historical Consciousness," in *The Ethos of History: Time and Responsibility*, edited by Stefan Helgesson and Jayne Svenungsson (New York: Berghahn, 2018), 32-53.

popular literature, established an explicit link between literary vampirism and Greekness. They chose Greek settings (ancient and modern) and drew on the modern Greek tradition, at least in the case of Byron, who, in his famous footnote to *The Giaour*, admits to have personally witnessed the consequences of vampire beliefs during his travels "in the Levant".[1] Other authors of the period, such as Robert Southey, who introduced a vampire in *Thalaba the Destroyer* (1801), also relied on accounts of the *vrykolakas*.[2] A few years later, in 1819, the creature became a mass-culture phenomenon following the publication of John William Polidori's *The Vampyre: A Tale*, a narrative not only partially set in Greece, but produced in the wake of—though noticeably against—Byron's previous engagements and obviously connected to the Philhellenic wave sweeping Europe at the time. Remarkably, it was this novel featuring Greek vampirism that shaped for the first time the modern archetype of the undead which would crystallize later, through *Dracula* and its cinematic adaptations, in the universal imagination.

Stories about the Greek undead, in sum, were no marginal subgenre in early vampire fiction. On the contrary, they constituted the main trunk of the rising genre. Why have they been forgotten, then? Why are we today totally unaware of their existence? Why, how, and when were Greek fictional vampires marginalized, excluded from the canon, and finally abandoned by authors?

Purging the Greek vampire: oblivion, displacement and the (short) way to Transylvania

This collection illustrates a part of this process while at the

1 Byron, *The Giaour: A Fragment of a Turkish Tale* (London: John Murray, 1813), 23.
2 Southey felt compelled to explain what a vampire was to his readers, who were certainly still unfamiliar with the term, so he included an extensive endnote transcribing two of the most popular 18th-century sources on vampirism: an Austrian surgeon's 1732 report on the vampire epidemic in a Serbian village, and the Frenchman Joseph Pitton de Tournefort's 1717 account of a case in the Greek island of Mykonos. See Robert Southey, *The Poetical Works*, vol. IV (London: Longman, 1821), 108-118.

same time recovering a precious legacy hitherto completely neglected. We start by reprinting the two foundational pieces of modern vampire fiction, Byron's "Fragment of a Novel" and Polidori's *The Vampyre*, both set in Greece and published in 1819 after having originated in the legendary, almost infinitely recreated "Gothic night" of June 1816 at Villa Diodati. The resounding success of the latter throughout Western Europe spawned a swarm of narrative and theatrical sequels that unleashed a true vampire craze on the continent during the 1820s. And it was precisely in the aftermath of that success that, due to the geopolitical circumstances of the era and to the cultural assumptions increasingly articulating Western identity, the machinery of suspicion was set in motion which finally led to the displacement of the literary vampire to spaces more befitting to heinous monstrosity. Very significantly, in May 1821 an anonymous critic of the Irish journal *The Stage* reproached the English theatrical version of Polidori's novel, James Planché's *The Vampire*, for giving vampirism a Hellenic location:

> The scene—the early part of the scene—is Athens; but the superstition is not Athenian, is not Grecian: There are no vampires in the splendid mythology of the ancients, rich as they are in the various and strange combinations of superstition. It is altogether a Turkish—an Oriental superstition. [...] Even were the scene laid in Greece, our youthful recollections of the *kalon kai agathon* [...] would revolt from the foul association. The scene should be laid among the followers of Islamism; and mosques and Oriental verandas should have supplied the place of basaltic caverns and gothic halls.[1]

Since the mid-18th century, an idealized image of (classical) Greece had been meticulously fabricated to work as the cradle of the modern West. This imaginary Greece, buttressed by aesthetic neoclassicism and the emergent discipline of the Classics, was essentially conceived as a paragon of harmony,

1 "The Vampire", *The Stage* I: XXVIII (Dublin, May 10, 1821), 109.

beauty, and rationalism. In other words, it epitomized the values that European culture—during a period of reorganization of the world's "mental map"—wanted to make its spiritual core in an effort to stand apart from a number of developing Others. This rampant Graecomania, central to the West's self-perception for decades, informed at the beginning of the nineteenth century a cultural and political movement that appealed to most sections of society: Philhellenism. Philhellenism advocated the national liberation of the Greek-speaking communities of the Ottoman Empire on account of their purported genealogical connection with the ancient Hellenes. As Greeks, despite some appearances, they were truly Europeans (at least deep inside), and accordingly they could not remain any longer under Turkish, Oriental rule. Furthermore, the hope arose that with their national regeneration a resurrection of the ancient Hellenic spirit would come about that would reinvigorate Western civilization. Greekness became thus an overly sweeping term designating a putative cultural continuum from Homer to modern-day Orthodox populations of Southeastern Europe.

Now, the problem came when those supposedly Greek populations, with all the historical accretions attached to the word, were observed to entertain such "horrible beliefs" as vampirism, "one of the most extraordinary and most revolting superstitions which ever disturbed the brains of any semi-barbarous people".[1] How could the representatives of the sublime Hellenic spirit, the highest of human civilizations, be the bearers of these brutal barbaric traditions? No wonder that the critic of *The Stage* was outraged at the bewildering conflation. For him (and for many of his contemporaries), Greece was substantially Ancient Greece, even when it was modern. Led by his preconceptions, he instinctively solved the dilemma by redrawing the geographical and cultural boundaries around the vampire: as a brutal belief, it belonged among Europe's (and Hellenism's) Others, that is, in the Orient. It

1 D., "On Vampyres," *New Monthly Magazine* VII (1823), 142.

should be "laid among the followers of Islamism": among the Turks.

This feeling must have been general in the 1820s. A few months before the piece in *The Stage* was published, in March 1821, an insurrection broke out among the Greeks of the East, marking the beginning of the Greek War of Independence. As the culmination of all Philhellenic hopes, it stirred up the enthusiasm of most Europeans. Philhellenism was at its peak. Many young Westerners voluntarily enlisted to fight the Ottomans on the ground and help Greece revive (do not miss the vampiric undertones of this expression) as a European nation. At this juncture, it was critical for propaganda to depict modern Greeks as fully Western subjects, worthy of the Hellenic legacy they carried on their shoulders. Vampirism, a savage tradition of blood-thirsty horror, upset this idyllic image of classicist harmony and, still worse, could taint Greekness, the cultural cradle of the West, with "oriental" accretions that would disrupt the genealogical narrative underpinning modern European identity. Although Byron had conceived the vampire as an instrument of Philhellenic propaganda intended to allegorize the brutal consequences of Turkish tyranny over Greece, Polidori's more persistent association of the undead with modern Greek traditions, even with Philhellenism itself,[1] made it imperative to cleanse Greekness from any monstrous or "Gothicizing" quality.

That is why Greek vampires, or the Greek origin of vampirism, gradually disappeared from fiction. Already in the 1820s, most of the extremely successful theatrical or novelistic adaptations of Polidori's *The Vampyre* marginalized the Greek episodes—not showing them on stage or relegating them to minor interspersed narrations—or, more frequently,

---

1 For this issue, see Matthew Gibson, *Dracula and the Eastern Question: British and French Vampire Narratives of the Nineteenth-Century Near East* (Basingstoke: Palgrave, 2006), 15-41 and my "The Pitfalls of Resurrection: Disquieting Hellenicities by the Time of the Greek Revolution," in *Periferias de la Revolución: Contextos transnacionales de la insurrección griega de 1821*, edited by Álvaro García Marín and Eva Latorre Broto (Madrid: ACHH, 2021), 401-404.

substituted other places, principally Scotland or Hungary, for Greece. Throughout the following decades, the process intensified, increasingly shrinking the vampire's Greek constituent. Symptomatic of this tendency is Alexandre Dumas's 1849 *The Thousand and One Ghosts*, where Kostaki, the undead that terrorizes the Polish narrator in the Carpathians, is just a quarter Greek.

The de-Hellenization of the vampire was achieved through two different strategies: (1) internalization, making the creature a member of the home society and, thus, an incarnation of intra-European class, economic, or sexual Otherness (for example, in *Varney the Vampire* [1845-47] or Waif Wander's "The White Maniac" [1867]); and, mainly, (2) relocation to more easily "otherizable" spaces placed beyond civilization or on the edge of civilization, especially Eastern Europe (Styria, Moldavia, Serbia, the Carpathians or, finally, Transylvania). By 1897, when *Dracula* gave the contemporary myth of the fictional vampire its universal form, every trace of Greekness had been completely removed from the collective mind. You will not find a single reference to Modern Greece in Stoker's novel. Curiously enough, though, the Modern Greek vampire continued to have a major presence in ethnological studies well into the twentieth century. Which means a certain censorship was in place for fiction that did not work for scholarship. At stake was the symbolic preservation of Greekness in the global social imagination—largely shaped by popular fiction in modern times—as the cultural soul of Western civilization.

A forgotten path to nowhere: post-1820 Greek vampires in English fiction

Before total eradication, however, a small number of stories still featured the Greek vampire in different manners. Published between 1829 and 1846, they form the main body of this volume, apart from Byron and Polidori's foundational pieces. Significantly, all of them appeared as part of non-literary genres (travel accounts) or in minor publication forms targeting "minor" audiences—always in the period's terms—such as children or women: gift books, magazines and juvenile moral books. Nor is it a coincidence that none of them made it into the canon of vampire fiction, even if a few of them, as I will briefly remark, could reasonably claim a place as true milestones of the genre. To be accurate, in fact, not only did they stay out of the canon: at least four of the five remain completely unknown today even to researchers and appear here for the first time since their original publication in the nineteenth century. Their traces were entirely lost on account of their dealing with a subject banished—or at least displaced—from the conventions of the modern myth. From that point of view, this book, in good vampire-hunter manner, comes to unearth a bunch of undead bodies—only not to put them to eternal rest, but hopefully quite the opposite.

While resisting the removal of the Greek vampire from fiction, all these pieces display complex strategies to negotiate the creature's position and make it conform to the new tacit "order". In this sense, they are the perfect embodiment of this process of proscription, showing at work some of the different compromises the Greek dimension of vampirism went through before its final extinction. Let us briefly go, to conclude, over their circumstances and operations.

Published during the Greek War of Independence, when Philhellenism was at its height, James Emerson Tennent's "Vampire of Santorini" (1829) works hard to "occidentalize" Greek folklore and, accordingly, Greece itself. Not only does he romanticize the supposedly traditional story, at least reshaped—if not wholly made up— by the author's hand as regards its narrative structure; he goes even further, and tries to exonerate Greece of the brutal dimension inherent in Slavic vampirism. Right before the story, Emerson Tennent takes care to remark that "this popular superstition […] varies from the vampire tales of Hungary in the demons being merely attached to mischief and not addicted to blood". As long as they are Greek, the *vrykolakes* need to be a milder, less monstrous, more humane version of the blood-thirsty revenants of the East. In order to save Modern Greece's "Westernness" on the eve of its independence, the author suggests that its vampires are of a distinct quality consistent with the Classics' idealized image of Hellenic culture. The narrative of Demetrio Gkikas, the reader will easily appreciate, seeks actively to corroborate this claim.

Throughout the 1830s and '40s, once Greece had become an independent nation-state, the approach varied slightly. The anonymous "The Vampire Knight" (1837), John Bowring's chapter on "Vampires" (1839), and James K. Paulding's "The Vroucolacas: A Tale" are conceived as Orientalist fantasies rather than as full-fledged horror stories. At different levels, their plot disempowers, "de-gothicizes" and domesticates the Greek undead by presenting it as a comical human fiction, a superstitious belief confined to the Orient. In this way, Greek vampirism is "refolklorized," detached from the domain of Gothic fiction with its totalizing, global-threatening monsters, and reframed in a provincial, exotic milieu. Moreover, in the new geopolitical context marked by the Eastern Question, where Modern Greece was increasingly seen with suspicion by the European powers, these narratives point at the new nation as a mere member of the Orient that shares with its neighbors all their signs of backwardness and Otherness: superstition, depravity, and an irritating inclination to deceit and treachery. The ultimate purpose of this depiction, I contend, is to disengage Modern Greece from the prestigious, transhistorical notion of Greekness that articulates Western identity, and thus save the latter from unsettling, anti-Hellenic conceptions such as vampirism.

On the other side, the anonymous "The Vampire of Vourla" (1845), the true gem of the collection, recuperates the Gothic potential of the Greek vampire to hint at the disturbing dimensions of Greekness, both ancient and modern, and especially at the dangers lurking in the multifaceted relationship between the West and the Hellenic, as Polidori's *The Vampyre* did—not by chance, in "Vourla", like in the latter, the evil triumphs and the fiend is never put to rest. It is inconceivable that this brilliant piece of vampire fiction has been lost for almost 180 years. Undoubtedly, its portrayal of conventional, predatory vampirism in a Greek setting is to blame for this oblivion. Otherwise, it would appear as a milestone of the genre, not only thanks to its outstanding quality and the fascinating character of the vampiric femme fatale it features, but also because it could arguably allow us to rewrite the whole history of vampire fiction in the 19th century. This might seem a bit of an overstatement, but "The Vampire of Vourla" anticipates a number of characteristics purportedly incorporated into the modern vampire myth for the first time by Bram Stoker's *Dracula*, fifty years later. The most important of these, without any doubt, is the ability of the vampire to transform itself into a bat and suck its victim's blood in that guise, hitherto thought to have been introduced at least in the 1880s.[1]

In sum, this collection will hopefully allow the reader to enjoy a set of magnificent stories unknown to this very day while, at the same time, completing the puzzle of vampire fiction with a precious missing piece obscured by the ubiquitous shadow of *Dracula* and its cinematic progeny.

Álvaro García Marín

Álvaro García Marín is an Assistant Professor of Translation and Interpretation at the University of Málaga (Spain). He has previously taught at Columbia University (New York) and the University of Seville (Spain), and has worked as a researcher at the Spanish National Research Council (Consejo Superior de Investigaciones Científicas, Madrid, Spain). He specializes in Modern Greek studies and the vampire in history and literature. Among his publications are the book *Historias del vampiro griego ([Hi]stories of the Greek Vampire*, 2017, in Spanish) and several papers in international books and journals.

1 See Kevin Dodd, "Blood Suckers Most Cruel: The Vampire and the Bat in and before Dracula," in *Athens Journal of Humanities & Arts* 6: 2 (2019), 107-132.

FRAGMENT OF A NOVEL (1819)

Lord Byron

George Gordon Byron (1788-1824), a lover of Greece and the Levant and the most successful writer of his age in Europe, was probably mainly responsible for the worldwide popularity of Philhellenism in the 1820s. He travelled extensively through the East and got to know first-hand lands still inaccessible to the majority of people, which he portrayed in romantic poems full of exotic color and wild passions. In 1813, he engaged for the first time with the Greek vrykolakas *in* The Giaour, *in the context of Philhellenic denunciation, in a passage where a Turkish pasha cursed the Christian protagonist to become a vampire after his death.*

Three years later, in the famous "ghost story challenge" of the summer of 1816 at Villa Diodati (Geneva, Switzerland), Byron produced the following cryptic story, which remained unfinished. It became the basis for the successful The Vampyre *(1819) by John William Polidori, his personal doctor, also a participant in that legendary night. Byron had not intended to publish the text, but in 1819 asked his publisher, John Murray, to do so with the purpose of dispelling the false idea that he was the author of Polidori's novel. So the "Fragment" came out in the same year as an appendix to the poem* Mazeppa. *Given its incomplete nature, we cannot know how vampirism was going to manifest in the text. We can only deduce that, while framed by the Greek tradition of the* vrykolakas, *undeadness is here more of a Turkish issue. Though apparently English, Darvell, the prospective vampire, is obviously related to the Ottomans. The piece thus suggests that the monster, a disguised Turk, will prey upon both Greece and the West.*

17

IN the year 17—, having for some time determined on a journey through countries not hitherto much frequented by travellers, I set out, accompanied by a friend, whom I shall designate by the name of Augustus Darvell. He was a few years my elder, and a man of considerable fortune and ancient family—advantages which an extensive capacity prevented him alike from undervaluing or overrating. Some peculiar circumstances in his private history had rendered him to me an object of attention, of interest, and even of regard, which neither the reserve of his manners, nor occasional indications of an inquietude at times nearly approaching to alienation of mind, could extinguish.

I was yet young in life, which I had begun early; but my intimacy with him was of a recent date: we had been educated at the same schools and university; but his progress through these had preceded mine, and he had been deeply initiated into what is called the world, while I was yet in my noviciate. While thus engaged, I had heard much both of his past and present life; and although in these accounts there were many and irreconcileable contradictions, I could still gather from the whole that he was a being of no common order, and one who, whatever pains he might take to avoid remark, would still be remarkable. I had cultivated his acquaintance subsequently, and endeavoured to obtain his friendship, but this last appeared to be unattainable; whatever affections he might have possessed seemed now, some to have been extinguished, and others to be concentred: that his feelings were acute, I had sufficient opportunities of observing; for, although he could control, he could not altogether disguise them: still he had a power of giving to one passion the appearance of another in such a manner that it was difficult to define the nature of what was working within him; and the expressions of his features would vary so rapidly, though slightly, that it was useless to trace them to their sources. It was evident that he was a prey to some cureless disquiet; but whether it arose from ambition, love, remorse, grief, from one or all of these, or merely from a morbid temperament akin to disease, I could not discover: there were circumstances alleged, which might have justified the application to each of these causes; but, as I have before said, these were so contradictory and contradicted, that none could be fixed upon with accuracy. Where there is mystery, it is generally supposed that there must also be evil: I know not how this may be, but in him there certainly was the one, though I could not ascertain the extent of the other—and felt loth, as far as regarded himself, to believe in its existence. My advances were received with sufficient coldness; but I was young, and not easily discouraged, and at length succeeded in obtaining, to a certain degree, that common-place intercourse and moderate confidence of common and every day concerns, created and cemented by similarity of pursuit and frequency of meeting, which is called intimacy, or friendship, according to the ideas of him who uses those words to express them.

Darvell had already travelled extensively; and to him I had applied for information with regard to the conduct of my intended journey. It was my secret wish that he might be prevailed on to accompany me: it was also a probable hope, founded upon the shadowy restlessness which I had observed in him, and to which the animation which he appeared to feel on such subjects, and his apparent indifference to all by which he was more immediately surrounded, gave fresh strength. This wish I first hinted, and then expressed: his answer, though I had partly expected it, gave me all the pleasure of surprise— he consented; and, after the requisite arrangements, we commenced our voyages. After journeying through various countries of the south of Europe, our attention was turned towards the East, according to our original destination; and it was in my progress through those regions that the incident occurred upon which will turn what I may have to relate.

The constitution of Darvell, which must from his appear-ance have been in early life more than usually robust, had been for some time gradually giving way, without the intervention of any apparent disease: he had neither cough nor hectic, yet he became daily more enfeebled: his habits were temperate, and he neither declined nor complained of fatigue, yet he was evidently wasting away: he became more and more silent and sleepless, and at length so seriously altered, that my alarm grew proportionate to what I conceived to be his danger.

We had determined, on our arrival at Smyrna, on an excursion to the ruins of Ephesus and Sardis, from which I endeavoured to dissuade him in his present state of indispo-sition—but in vain: there appeared to be an oppression on his mind, and a solemnity in his manner, which ill corresponded with his eagerness to proceed on what I regarded as a mere party of pleasure, little suited to a valetudinarian; but I opposed him no longer—and in a few days we set off together, accompanied only by a serrugee and a single janizary.

We had passed halfway towards the remains of Ephesus, leaving behind us the more fertile environs of Smyrna, and were entering upon that wild and tenantless track through the marshes and defiles which lead to the few huts yet lingering over the broken columns of Diana—the roofless walls of expelled Christianity, and the still more recent but complete desolation of abandoned mosques—when the sudden and rapid illness of my companion obliged us to halt at a Turkish cemetery, the turbaned tombstones of which were the sole indication that human life had ever been a sojourner in this wilderness. The only caravansera we had seen was left some hours behind us, not a vestige of a town or even cottage was within sight or hope, and this "city of the dead" appeared to be the sole refuge for my unfortunate friend, who seemed on the verge of becoming the last of its inhabitants.

In this situation, I looked round for a place where he might most conveniently repose:—contrary to the usual aspect of

Mahometan burial-grounds, the cypresses were in this few in number, and these thinly scattered over its extent: the tomb-stones were mostly fallen, and worn with age:—upon one of the most considerable of these, and beneath one of the most spreading trees, Darvell supported himself, in a half-reclining posture, with great difficulty. He asked for water. I had some doubts of our being able to find any, and prepared to go in search of it with hesitating despondency—but he desired me to remain; and turning to Suleiman, our janizary, who stood by us smoking with great tranquillity, he said, "Suleiman, verbana su," (i. e. bring some water,) and went on describing the spot where it was to be found with great minuteness, at a small well for camels, a few hundred yards to the right: the janizary obeyed. I said to Darvell, "How did you know this?"—He replied, "From our situation; you must perceive that this place was once inhabited, and could not have been so without springs: I have also been here before."

"You have been here before!—How came you never to mention this to me? and what could you be doing in a place where no one would remain a moment longer than they could help it?"

To this question I received no answer. In the mean time Suleiman returned with the water, leaving the serrugee and the horses at the fountain. The quenching of his thirst had the appearance of reviving him for a moment; and I conceived hopes of his being able to proceed, or at least to return, and I urged the attempt. He was silent—and appeared to be collecting his spirits for an effort to speak. He began.

"This is the end of my journey, and of my life—I came here to die: but I have a request to make, a command—for such my last words must be—You will observe it?"

"Most certainly; but have better hopes."

"I have no hopes, nor wishes, but this—conceal my death from every human being."

"I hope there will be no occasion; that you will recover, and——"

"Peace!—it must be so: promise this."

"I do."

"Swear it, by all that"——He here dictated an oath of great solemnity.

"There is no occasion for this—I will observe your request; and to doubt me is——"

"It cannot be helped,—you must swear."

I took the oath: it appeared to relieve him. He removed a seal ring from his finger, on which were some Arabic characters, and presented it to me. He proceeded—

"On the ninth day of the month, at noon precisely (what month you please, but this must be the day), you must fling this ring into the salt springs which run into the Bay of Eleusis: the day after, at the same hour, you must repair to the ruins of the temple of Ceres, and wait one hour."

"Why?"

"You will see."

"The ninth day of the month, you say?"

"The ninth."

As I observed that the present was the ninth day of the month, his countenance changed, and he paused. As he sate, evidently becoming more feeble, a stork, with a snake in her beak, perched upon a tombstone near us; and, without devouring her prey, appeared to be stedfastly regarding us. I know not what impelled me to drive it away, but the attempt was useless; she made a few circles in the air, and returned exactly to the same spot. Darvell pointed to it, and smiled: he spoke—I know not whether to himself or to me—but the words were only, " 'Tis well!"

"What is well? what do you mean?"

"No matter: you must bury me here this evening, and exactly where that bird is now perched. You know the rest of my injunctions."

He then proceeded to give me several directions as to the manner in which his death might be best concealed. After these were finished, he exclaimed, "You perceive that bird?"

"Certainly."

"And the serpent writhing in her beak?"

"Doubtless: there is nothing uncommon in it; it is her natural prey. But it is odd that she does not devour it."

He smiled in a ghastly manner, and said, faintly, "It is not yet time!" As he spoke, the stork flew away. My eyes followed it for a moment, it could hardly be longer than ten might be counted. I felt Darvell's weight, as it were, increase upon my shoulder, and, turning to look upon his face, perceived that he was dead.

I was shocked with the sudden certainty which could not be mistaken—his countenance in a few minutes became nearly black. I should have attributed so rapid a change to poison, had I not been aware that he had no opportunity of receiving it unperceived. The day was declining, the body was rapidly altering, and nothing remained but to fulfil his request. With the aid of Suleiman's ataghan and my own sabre, we scooped a shallow grave upon the spot which Darvell had indicated: the earth easily gave way, having already received some Mahometan tenant. We dug as deeply as the time permitted us, and throwing the dry earth upon all that remained of the singular being so lately departed, we cut a few sods of greener turf from the less withered soil around us, and laid them upon his sepulchre.

Between astonishment and grief, I was tearless. * * * * *

THE VAMPYRE: A TALE (1819)
John William Polidori

During the "ghost story challenge" on that mythic summer night in 1816 in Geneva, John Polidori (1795-1821), "poor Polidori" in Mary Shelley's words, came up with "some terrible idea about a skull-headed lady." A few months earlier, he had entered Lord Byron's service as his personal physician with the purpose of accompanying the poet on his trip through Europe. Their tortuous relationship, full of envy and resentment—especially on Polidori's part—, ended in September of the same year, when Byron dismissed him. Three years later, still harboring literary ambitions and eager to take revenge on his former employer, Polidori wrote The Vampyre *"in three mornings", as he admits, "at the request of a lady". The narrative was clearly based on Byron's "Fragment of a Novel," which he skillfully reshaped to make the vampire an alter ego of the illustrious poet, a wandering and unscrupulous aristocrat who takes advantage of people around him by metaphorically draining their life. To Polidori's dismay, the book was initially published as Lord Byron's, and it took some time to clear up the confusion. Apparently, this whole affair played a role in young Polidori's depression and subsequent suicide. However, the spectacular success of the novel throughout Europe marked the monster's definitive transition to mass cultural phenomenon and fashioned its modern fictional archetype.*

Polidori drew from the Greek tradition of the vrykolakas *and set his narrative in Modern Greece. In a sense, besides a condemnation of Byron, the tale can be read as an anti-Philhellenic allegory warning the West against the dangers of an excessive cultural infatuation with Greekness. Ruthven, a Philhellene like Byron, is a hybrid English-Greek vampire who attacks and eventually destroys both*

Greeks and Westerners. So vampirism, in truth, emerges not from the primeval traditions of the Hellenic land, but from the cultural contact between the colonialist gaze of the Western cosmopolite—who is also a classicist or an antiquarian—and the contemporary reality of the country.

INTRODUCTION.

THE superstition upon which this tale is founded is very general in the East. Among the Arabians it appears to be common: it did not, however, extend itself to the Greeks until after the establishment of Christianity; and it has only assumed its present form since the division of the Latin and Greek churches; at which time, the idea becoming prevalent, that a Latin body could not corrupt if buried in their territory, it gradually increased, and formed the subject of many wonderful stories, still extant, of the dead rising from their graves, and feeding upon the blood of the young and beautiful. In the West it spread, with some slight variation, all over Hungary, Poland, Austria, and Lorraine, where the belief existed, that vampyres nightly imbibed a certain portion of the blood of their victims, who became emaciated, lost their strength, and speedily died of consumptions; whilst these human blood-suckers fattened—and their veins became distended to such a state of repletion, as to cause the blood to flow from all the passages of their bodies, and even from the very pores of their skins.

In the London Journal, of March, 1732, is a curious, and, of course, *credible* account of a particular case of vampyrism, which is stated to have occurred at Madreyga, in Hungary. It appears, that upon an examination of the commander-in-chief and magistrates of the place, they positively and unanimously affirmed, that, about five years before, a certain Heyduke, named Arnold Paul, had been heard to say, that, at Cassovia, on the frontiers of the Turkish Servia, he had been tormented by a vampyre, but had found a way to rid himself of the evil, by eating some of the earth out of the vampyre's grave, and rubbing himself with his blood. This precaution, however, did not prevent him from becoming a vampyre[1] himself; for, about twenty or thirty days after his death and burial, many persons complained of having been tormented by him, and a deposition was made, that four persons had been deprived of life by his attacks. To prevent further mischief, the inhabitants having consulted their Hadagni,[2] took up the body, and found it (as is supposed to be usual in cases of vampyrism) fresh, and entirely free from corruption, and emitting at the mouth, nose, and ears, pure and florid blood. Proof having been thus obtained, they resorted to the accustomed remedy. A stake was driven entirely through the heart and body of Arnold Paul, at which he is reported to have cried out as dreadfully as if he had been alive. This done, they cut off his head, burned his body, and threw the ashes into his grave. The same measures were adopted with the corses of those persons who had previously died from vampyrism, lest they should, in their turn, become agents upon others who survived them.

This monstrous rodomontade is here related, because it seems better adapted to illustrate the subject of the present observations than any other instance which could be adduced. In many parts of Greece it is considered as a sort of punishment after death, for some heinous crime committed whilst in existence, that the deceased is not only doomed to vampyrise, but compelled to confine his infernal visitations solely to those beings he loved most while upon earth—those to whom he was bound by ties of kindred and affection.—A supposition alluded to in the "Giaour."

> But first on earth, as Vampyre sent,
> Thy corse shall from its tomb be rent;
> Then ghastly haunt the native place,

1 The universal belief is, that a person sucked by a vampyre becomes a vampyre himself, and sucks in his turn.
2 Chief bailiff.

And suck the blood of all thy race;
There from thy *daughter, sister, wife,*
At midnight drain the stream of life;
Yet loathe the banquet which perforce
Must feed thy livid living corse,
Thy victims, ere they yet expire,
Shall know the demon for their sire;
As cursing thee, thou cursing them,
Thy flowers are withered on the stem.
But one that for *thy* crime must fall,
The youngest, best beloved of all,
Shall bless thee with a *father's* name—
That word shall wrap thy heart in flame?
Yet thou must end thy task and mark
Her cheek's last tinge—her eye's last spark,
And the last glassy glance must view
Which freezes o'er its lifeless blue;
Then with unhallowed hand shall tear
The tresses of her yellow hair,
Of which, in life a lock when shorn
Affection's fondest pledge was worn—
But now is borne away by thee
Memorial of thine agony!
Yet with thine own best blood shall drip;
Thy gnashing tooth, and haggard lip;
Then stalking to thy sullen grave,
Go—and with Gouls and Afrits rave,
Till these in horror shrink away
From spectre more accursed than they.

Mr. Southey has also introduced in his wild but beautiful poem of "Thalaba," the vampyre corse of the Arabian maid Oneiza, who is represented as having returned from the grave for the purpose of tormenting him she best loved whilst in existence. But this cannot be supposed to have resulted from the sinfulness of her life, she being pourtrayed throughout the whole of the tale as a complete type of purity and innocence. The veracious Tournefort gives a long account in his travels of several astonishing cases of vampyrism, to which he pretends to have been an eyewitness; and Calmet, in his great work upon this subject, besides a variety of anecdotes, and traditionary narratives illustrative of its effects, has put forth some learned dissertations, tending to prove it to be a classical, as well as barbarian error.

Many curious and interesting notices on this singularly horrible superstition might be added; though the present may suffice for the limits of a note, necessarily devoted to explanation, and which may now be concluded by merely remarking, that though the term Vampyre is the one in most general acceptation, there are several others synonymous with it, made use of in various parts of the world: as Vroucolocha, Vardoulacha, Goul, Broucoloka, &c.

THE VAMPYRE.

IT happened that in the midst of the dissipations attendant upon a London winter, there appeared at the various parties of the leaders of the *ton* a nobleman, more remarkable for his singularities, than his rank. He gazed upon the mirth around him, as if he could not participate therein. Apparently, the light laughter of the fair only attracted his attention, that he might by a look quell it, and throw fear into those breasts where thoughtlessness reigned. Those who felt this sensation of awe, could not explain whence it arose: some attributed it to the dead grey eye, which, fixing upon the object's face, did not seem to penetrate, and at one glance to pierce through to the inward workings of the heart; but fell upon the cheek with a leaden ray that weighed upon the skin it could not pass. His peculiarities caused him to be invited to every house; all wished to see him, and those who had been accustomed to violent excitement, and now felt the weight of *ennui*, were pleased at having something in their presence capable of engaging their attention. In spite of the deadly hue of his face, which never gained a warmer tint, either from the blush of modesty, or from the strong emotion of passion, though its form and outline were beautiful, many of the female hunters after notoriety attempted to win his attentions, and gain, at least, some marks of what they might term affection: Lady Mercer, who had been the mockery of every monster shewn in drawing-rooms since her marriage, threw herself in his way, and did all but put on the dress of a mountebank, to attract his notice:—though in vain:—when she stood before him, though his eyes were apparently fixed upon her's, still it seemed as if they were unperceived;—even her unappalled impudence was baffled, and she left the field. But though the common adultress could not influence even the guidance of his eyes, it was not that the female sex was indifferent to him: yet such was the apparent caution with which he spoke to the virtuous wife and innocent daughter, that few knew he ever addressed himself to females. He had, however, the reputation of a winning tongue; and whether it was that it even overcame the dread of his singular character, or that they were moved by his apparent hatred of vice, he was as often among those females who form the boast of their sex from their domestic virtues, as among those who sully it by their vices.

About the same time, there came to London a young gentleman of the name of Aubrey: he was an orphan left with an only sister in the possession of great wealth, by parents who died while he was yet in childhood. Left also to himself by guardians, who thought it their duty merely to take care of his fortune, while they relinquished the more important charge of his mind to the care of mercenary subalterns, he cultivated more his imagination than his judgment. He had, hence, that high romantic feeling of honour and candour, which daily ruins so many milliners' apprentices. He believed all to sympathise with virtue, and thought that vice was thrown in by Providence merely for the picturesque effect of the scene, as we see in romances: he thought that the misery of a cottage merely consisted in the vesting of clothes, which were as warm, but which were better adapted to the painter's eye by their irregular folds and various coloured patches. He thought, in fine, that the dreams of poets were the realities of life. He was handsome, frank, and rich: for these reasons, upon his entering into the gay circles, many mothers surrounded him, striving which should describe with least truth their languishing or romping favourites: the daughters at the same time, by their brightening countenances when he approached, and by their sparkling eyes, when he opened his lips, soon led him into false notions of his talents and his merit. Attached as he was to the romance of his solitary hours, he was startled at finding, that, except in the tallow and wax candles that flickered, not from the presence of a ghost, but from want of snuffing, there was no foundation in real life for any of that congeries of pleasing pictures and descriptions contained in those volumes, from which he had formed his study. Finding, however, some compensation in his gratified vanity, he was about to relinquish his dreams, when the extraordinary being we have above described, crossed him in his career.

He watched him; and the very impossibility of forming an idea of the character of a man entirely absorbed in himself, who gave few other signs of his observation of external objects, than the tacit assent to their existence, implied by the avoidance of their contact: allowing his imagination to picture every thing that flattered its propensity to extravagant ideas, he soon formed this object into the hero of a romance, and determined to observe the offspring of his fancy, rather than the person before him. He became acquainted with him, paid him attentions, and so far advanced upon his notice, that his presence was always recognised. He gradually learnt that Lord Ruthven's affairs were embarrassed, and soon found, from the notes of preparation in —— Street, that he was about to travel. Desirous of gaining some information respecting this singular character, who, till now, had only whetted his curiosity, he hinted to his guardians, that it was time for him to perform the tour, which for many generations has been thought necessary to enable the young to take some rapid steps in the career of vice towards putting themselves upon an equality with the aged, and not allowing them to appear as if fallen from the skies, whenever scandalous intrigues are mentioned as the subjects of pleasantry or of praise, according to the degree of skill shewn in carrying them on. They consented: and Aubrey immediately mentioning his intentions to Lord Ruthven, was surprised to receive from him a proposal to join him. Flattered by such a mark of esteem from him, who, apparently, had nothing in common with other men, he gladly accepted it, and in a few days they had passed the circling waters.

Hitherto, Aubrey had had no opportunity of studying Lord Ruthven's character, and now he found, that, though many more of his actions were exposed to his view, the results offered different conclusions from the apparent motives to his conduct. His companion was profuse in his liberality;—the idle, the vagabond, and the beggar, received from his hand more than enough to relieve their immediate wants. But Aubrey could not avoid remarking, that it was not upon the virtuous, reduced to indigence by the misfortunes attendant even upon virtue, that he bestowed his alms;—these were sent from the door with hardly suppressed sneers; but when the profligate came to ask something, not to relieve his wants, but to allow him to wallow in his lust, or to sink him still deeper in his iniquity, he was sent away with rich charity. This was, however, attributed by him to the greater importunity of the vicious, which generally prevails over the retiring bashfulness of the virtuous indigent. There was one circumstance about the charity of his Lordship, which was still more impressed upon his mind: all those upon whom it was bestowed, inevitably found that there was a curse upon it, for they were all either led to the scaffold, or sunk to the lowest and the most abject misery. At Brussels and other towns through which they passed, Aubrey was surprized at the apparent eagerness with which his companion sought for the centres of all fashionable vice; there he entered into all the spirit of the faro table: he betted, and always gambled with success, except where the known sharper was his antagonist, and then he lost even more than he gained; but it was always with the same unchanging face, with which he generally watched the society around: it was not, however, so when he encountered the rash youthful novice, or the luckless father of a numerous family; then his very wish seemed fortune's law—this apparent abstractedness of mind was laid aside, and his eyes sparkled with more fire than that of the cat whilst dallying with the half-dead mouse. In every town, he left the formerly affluent youth, torn from the circle he adorned, cursing, in the solitude of a dungeon, the fate that had drawn him within the reach of this fiend; whilst many a father sat frantic, amidst the speaking looks of mute hungry children, without a single farthing of his late immense wealth, wherewith to buy even sufficient to satisfy their present craving. Yet he took no money from the gambling table; but immediately lost, to the ruiner of many, the last gilder he had just snatched from the convulsive grasp of the innocent: this might but be the result of a certain degree of knowledge, which was not, however, capable of combating the cunning of the more experienced. Aubrey often wished to represent this to his friend, and beg him to resign that charity and pleasure which proved the ruin of all, and did not tend to his own profit;—but he delayed it—for each day he hoped his friend would give him some opportunity of speaking frankly and openly to him; however, this never occurred. Lord Ruthven in his carriage, and amidst the various wild and rich scenes of nature, was always the same: his eye spoke less than his lip; and though Aubrey was near the object of his curiosity, he obtained no greater gratification from it than the constant excitement of vainly wishing to break that mystery, which to his exalted imagination began to assume the appearance of something supernatural.

They soon arrived at Rome, and Aubrey for a time lost sight of his companion; he left him in daily attendance upon the morning circle of an Italian countess, whilst he went in search of the memorials of another almost deserted city. Whilst he was thus engaged, letters arrived from England, which he opened with eager impatience; the first was from his sister, breathing nothing but affection; the others were from his guardians, the latter astonished him; if it had before entered into his imagination that there was an evil power resident in his companion, these seemed to give him sufficient reason for the belief. His guardians insisted upon his immediately leaving his friend, and urged, that his character was dreadfully vicious, for that the possession of irresistible powers of seduction, rendered his licentious habits more dangerous to society. It had been discovered, that his contempt for the adultress had not originated in hatred of her character; but that he had required, to enhance his gratification, that his victim, the partner of his guilt, should be hurled from the pinnacle of unsullied virtue, down to the lowest abyss of infamy and degradation: in fine, that all those females whom he had sought, apparently on account of their virtue, had, since his departure, thrown even the mask aside, and had not scrupled to expose the whole deformity of their vices to the public gaze.

Aubrey determined upon leaving one, whose character had not yet shown a single bright point on which to rest the eye. He resolved to invent some plausible pretext for abandoning him altogether, purposing, in the mean while, to watch him more closely, and to let no slight circumstances pass by unnoticed. He entered into the same circle, and soon perceived, that his Lordship was endeavouring to work upon the inexperience of the daughter of the lady whose house he chiefly frequented. In Italy, it is seldom that an unmarried female is met with in society; he was therefore obliged to carry on his plans in secret; but Aubrey's eye followed him in all his windings, and soon discovered that an assignation had been appointed, which would most likely end in the ruin of an innocent, though thoughtless girl. Losing no time, he entered the apartment of Lord Ruthven, and abruptly asked him his intentions with respect to the lady, informing him at the same time that he was aware of his being about to meet her that very night. Lord Ruthven answered, that his intentions were such as he supposed all would have upon such an occasion; and upon being pressed whether he intended to marry her, merely laughed. Aubrey retired; and, immediately writing a note, to say, that from that moment he must decline accompanying his Lordship in the remainder of their proposed tour, he ordered his servant to seek other apartments, and calling upon the mother of the lady, informed her of all he knew, not only with regard to her daughter, but also concerning the character of his Lordship. The assignation was prevented. Lord Ruthven next day merely sent his servant to notify his complete assent to a separation; but did not hint any suspicion of his plans having been foiled by Aubrey's interposition.

Having left Rome, Aubrey directed his steps towards Greece, and crossing the Peninsula, soon found himself at Athens. He then fixed his residence in the house of a Greek; and soon occupied himself in tracing the faded records of ancient glory upon monuments that apparently, ashamed of chronicling the deeds of freemen only before slaves, had hidden themselves beneath the sheltering soil or many coloured lichen. Under the same roof as himself, existed a being, so beautiful and delicate, that she might have formed the model for a painter wishing to pourtray on canvass the promised hope of the faithful in Mahomet's paradise, save that her eyes spoke too much mind for any one to think she could belong to those who had no souls. As she danced upon the plain, or tripped along the mountain's side, one would have thought the gazelle a poor type of her beauties; for who would have exchanged her eye, apparently the eye of animated nature, for that sleepy luxurious look of the animal suited but to the taste of an epicure. The light step of Ianthe often accompanied Aubrey in his search after antiquities, and often would the unconscious girl, engaged in the pursuit of a Kashmere butterfly, show the whole beauty of her form, floating as it were upon the wind, to the eager gaze of him, who forgot the letters he had just decyphered upon an almost effaced tablet, in the contemplation of her sylph-like figure. Often would her tresses falling, as she flitted around, exhibit in the sun's ray such delicately brilliant and swiftly fading hues, it might well excuse the forgetfulness of the antiquary, who let escape from his mind the very object he had before thought of vital importance to the proper interpretation of a passage in Pausanias. But why attempt to describe charms which all feel, but none can appreciate?—It was innocence, youth, and beauty, unaffected by crowded drawing-rooms and stifling balls. Whilst he drew those remains of which he wished to preserve a memorial for his future hours, she would stand by, and watch the magic effects of his pencil, in tracing the scenes of her native place; she would then describe to him the circling dance upon the open plain, would paint to him in all the glowing colours of youthful memory, the marriage pomp she remembered viewing in her infancy; and then, turning to subjects that had evidently made a greater impression upon her mind, would tell him all the supernatural tales of her nurse. Her earnestness and apparent belief of what she narrated, excited the interest even of Aubrey; and often as she told him the tale of the living vampyre, who had passed years amidst his friends, and dearest ties, forced every year, by feeding upon the life of a lovely female to prolong his existence for the ensuing months, his blood would run cold, whilst he attempted to laugh her out of such idle and horrible fantasies; but Ianthe cited to him the names of old men, who had at last detected one living among themselves, after several of their near relatives and children had been found marked with the stamp of the fiend's appetite; and when she found him so incredulous, she begged of him to believe her, for it had been remarked, that those who had dared to question their existence, always had some proof given, which obliged them, with grief and heartbreaking, to confess it was true. She detailed to him the traditional appearance of these monsters, and his horror was increased, by hearing a pretty accurate description of Lord

Ruthven; he, however, still persisted in persuading her, that there could be no truth in her fears, though at the same time he wondered at the many coincidences which had all tended to excite a belief in the supernatural power of Lord Ruthven.

Aubrey began to attach himself more and more to Ianthe; her innocence, so contrasted with all the affected virtues of the women among whom he had sought for his vision of romance, won his heart; and while he ridiculed the idea of a young man of English habits, marrying an uneducated Greek girl, still he found himself more and more attached to the almost fairy form before him. He would tear himself at times from her, and, forming a plan for some antiquarian research, he would depart, determined not to return until his object was attained; but he always found it impossible to fix his attention upon the ruins around him, whilst in his mind he retained an image that seemed alone the rightful possessor of his thoughts. Ianthe was unconscious of his love, and was ever the same frank infantile being he had first known. She always seemed to part from him with reluctance; but it was because she had no longer any one with whom she could visit her favourite haunts, whilst her guardian was occupied in sketching or uncovering some fragment which had yet escaped the destructive hand of time. She had appealed to her parents on the subject of Vampyres, and they both, with several present, affirmed their existence, pale with horror at the very name. Soon after, Aubrey determined to proceed upon one of his excursions, which was to detain him for a few hours; when they heard the name of the place, they all at once begged of him not to return at night, as he must necessarily pass through a wood, where no Greek would ever remain, after the day had closed, upon any consideration. They described it as the resort of the vampyres in their nocturnal orgies, and denounced the most heavy evils as impending upon him who dared to cross their path. Aubrey made light of their representations, and tried to laugh them out of the idea; but when he saw them shudder at his daring thus to mock a superior, infernal power, the very name of which apparently made their blood freeze, he was silent.

Next morning Aubrey set off upon his excursion unattended; he was surprised to observe the melancholy face of his host, and was concerned to find that his words, mocking the belief of those horrible fiends, had inspired them with such terror. When he was about to depart, Ianthe came to the side of his horse, and earnestly begged of him to return, ere night allowed the power of these beings to be put in action;—he promised. He was, however, so occupied in his research, that he did not perceive that day-light would soon end, and that in the horizon there was one of those specks which, in the warmer climates, so rapidly gather into a tremendous mass, and pour all their rage upon the devoted country.—He at last, however, mounted his horse, determined to make up by speed for his delay: but it was too late. Twilight, in these southern climates, is almost unknown; immediately the sun sets, night begins: and ere he had advanced far, the power of the storm was above—its echoing thunders had scarcely an interval of rest—its thick heavy rain forced its way through the canopying foliage, whilst the blue forked lightning seemed to fall and radiate at his very feet. Suddenly his horse took fright, and he was carried with dreadful rapidity through the entangled forest. The animal at last, through fatigue, stopped, and he found, by the glare of lightning, that he was in the neighbourhood of a hovel that hardly lifted itself up from the masses of dead leaves and brushwood which surrounded it. Dismounting, he approached, hoping to find some one to guide him to the town, or at least trusting to obtain shelter from the pelting of the storm. As he approached, the thunders, for a moment silent, allowed him to hear the dreadful shrieks of a woman mingling with the stifled, exultant mockery of a laugh, continued in one almost unbroken sound;—he was startled: but, roused by the thunder which again rolled over his head, he, with a sudden effort, forced open the door of the hut. He found himself in utter darkness: the sound, however, guided him. He was apparently unperceived; for, though he called, still the sounds continued, and no notice was taken of him. He found himself in contact with some one, whom he immediately seized; when a voice cried, "Again baffled!" to which a loud laugh succeeded; and he felt himself grappled by one whose strength seemed superhuman: determined to sell his life as dearly as he could, he struggled; but it was in vain: he was lifted from his feet and hurled with enormous force against the ground:—his enemy threw himself upon him, and kneeling upon his breast, had placed his hands upon his throat—when the glare of many torches penetrating through the hole that gave light in the day, disturbed him;—he instantly rose, and, leaving his prey, rushed through the door, and in a moment the crashing of the branches, as he broke through the wood, was no longer heard. The storm was now still; and Aubrey, incapable of moving, was soon heard by those without. They entered; the light of their torches fell upon the mud walls, and the thatch loaded on every individual straw with heavy flakes of soot. At the desire of Aubrey they searched for her who had attracted him by her cries; he was again left in darkness; but what was his horror, when the light of the torches once more burst upon him, to perceive the airy form of his fair conductress brought in a lifeless corse. He shut his eyes, hoping that it was but a vision arising from his disturbed imagination; but he again saw the same form, when he unclosed them, stretched by his side. There was no colour upon her cheek, not even upon her lip; yet there was a stillness about her face that seemed almost as attaching as the life that once dwelt there:—upon her neck and breast was blood, and upon her throat were the marks of teeth having opened the vein:—to this the men pointed, crying, simultaneously struck with horror, "A Vampyre! a Vampyre!" A litter was quickly formed, and Aubrey was laid by the side of her who had lately been to him the object of so many bright and fairy visions, now fallen with the flower of life that had died within her. He knew not what his thoughts were—his mind was benumbed and seemed to shun reflection, and take refuge in vacancy—he held almost unconsciously in his hand a naked dagger of a particular construction, which had been found in the hut. They were soon met by different parties who had been engaged in the search of her whom a mother had missed. Their lamentable cries, as they approached the city, forewarned the parents of some dreadful catastrophe.—To describe their grief would be impossible; but when they ascertained the cause of their child's death, they looked at Aubrey, and pointed to the corse. They were inconsolable; both died broken-hearted.

Aubrey being put to bed was seized with a most violent fever, and was often delirious; in these intervals he would call upon Lord Ruthven and upon Ianthe—by some unaccountable combination he seemed to beg of his former companion to spare the being he loved. At other times he would imprecate maledictions upon his head, and curse him as her destroyer. Lord Ruthven chanced at this time to arrive at Athens, and, from whatever motive, upon hearing of the state of Aubrey, immediately placed himself in the same house, and became his constant attendant. When the latter recovered from his delirium, he was horrified and startled at the sight of him whose image he had now combined with that of a Vampyre; but Lord Ruthven, by his kind words, implying almost repentance for the fault that had caused their separation, and still more by the attention, anxiety, and care which he showed, soon reconciled him to his presence. His lordship seemed quite changed; he no longer appeared that apathetic being who had so astonished Aubrey; but as soon as his convalescence began to be rapid, he again gradually retired into the same state of mind, and Aubrey perceived no difference from the former man, except that at times he was surprised to meet his gaze fixed intently upon him, with a smile of malicious exultation playing upon his lips: he knew not why, but this smile haunted him. During the last stage of the invalid's recovery, Lord Ruthven was apparently engaged in watching the tideless waves raised by the cooling breeze, or in marking the progress of those orbs, circling, like our world, the moveless sun;—indeed, he appeared to wish to avoid the eyes of all.

Aubrey's mind, by this shock, was much weakened, and that elasticity of spirit which had once so distinguished him now seemed to have fled for ever. He was now as much a lover of solitude and silence as Lord Ruthven; but much as he wished for solitude, his mind could not find it in the neighbourhood of Athens; if he sought it amidst the ruins he had formerly frequented, Ianthe's form stood by his side—if he sought it in the woods, her light step would appear wandering amidst the underwood, in quest of the modest violet; then suddenly turning round, would show, to his wild imagination, her pale face and wounded throat, with a meek smile upon her lips. He determined to fly scenes, every feature of which created such bitter associations in his mind. He proposed to Lord Ruthven, to whom he held himself bound by the tender care he had taken of him during his illness, that they should visit those parts of Greece neither had yet seen. They travelled in every direction, and sought every spot to which a recollection could be attached: but though they thus hastened from place to place, yet they seemed not to heed what they gazed upon. They heard much of robbers, but they gradually began to slight these reports, which they imagined were only the invention of individuals, whose interest it was to excite the generosity of those whom they defended from pretended dangers. In consequence of thus neglecting the advice of the inhabitants, on one occasion they travelled with only a few guards, more to serve as guides than as a defence. Upon entering, however, a narrow defile, at the bottom of which was the bed of a torrent, with large masses of rock brought down from the neighbouring precipices, they had reason to repent their negligence; for scarcely were the whole of the party engaged in the narrow pass, when they were startled by the whistling of bullets close to their heads, and by the echoed report of several guns. In an instant their guards had left them, and, placing themselves behind rocks, had begun to fire in the direction whence the report came. Lord Ruthven and Aubrey, imitating their example, retired for a moment behind the sheltering turn of the defile: but ashamed of being thus detained by a foe, who with insulting shouts bade them advance, and being exposed to unresisting slaughter, if any of the robbers should climb above and take them in the rear, they determined at once to rush forward in search of the enemy. Hardly had they lost the shelter of the rock, when Lord Ruthven received a shot in the shoulder, which brought him to the ground. Aubrey hastened to his assistance; and, no longer heeding the contest or his own peril, was soon surprised by seeing the robbers' faces around him—his guards having, upon Lord Ruthven's being wounded, immediately thrown up their arms and surrendered.

By promises of great reward, Aubrey soon induced them to convey his wounded friend to a neighbouring cabin; and having agreed upon a ransom, he was no more disturbed by their presence—they being content merely to guard the entrance till their comrade should return with the promised sum, for which he had an order. Lord Ruthven's strength rapidly decreased; in two days mortification ensued, and death seemed advancing with hasty steps. His conduct and appearance had not changed; he seemed as unconscious of pain as he had been of the objects about him: but towards the close of the last evening, his mind became apparently uneasy, and his eye often fixed upon Aubrey, who was induced to offer his assistance with more than usual earnestness—"Assist me! you may save me—you may do more than that—I mean not my life, I heed the death of my existence as little as that of the passing day; but you may save my honour, your friend's honour."—"How? tell me how? I would do any thing," replied Aubrey.—"I need but little—my life ebbs apace—I cannot explain the whole—but if you would conceal all you know of me, my honour were free from stain in the world's mouth—and if my death were unknown for some time in England—I—I—but life."—"It shall not be known."—"Swear!"

cried the dying man, raising himself with exultant violence, "Swear by all your soul reveres, by all your nature fears, swear that, for a year and a day you will not impart your knowledge of my crimes or death to any living being in any way, whatever may happen, or whatever you may see."—His eyes seemed bursting from their sockets: "I swear!" said Aubrey; he sunk laughing upon his pillow, and breathed no more.

Aubrey retired to rest, but did not sleep; the many circumstances attending his acquaintance with this man rose upon his mind, and he knew not why; when he remembered his oath a cold shivering came over him, as if from the presentiment of something horrible awaiting him. Rising early in the morning, he was about to enter the hovel in which he had left the corpse, when a robber met him, and informed him that it was no longer there, having been conveyed by himself and comrades, upon his retiring, to the pinnacle of a neighbouring mount, according to a promise they had given his lordship, that it should be exposed to the first cold ray of the moon that rose after his death. Aubrey astonished, and taking several of the men, determined to go and bury it upon the spot where it lay. But, when he had mounted to the summit he found no trace of either the corpse or the clothes, though the robbers swore they pointed out the identical rock on which they had laid the body. For a time his mind was bewildered in conjectures, but he at last returned, convinced that they had buried the corpse for the sake of the clothes.

Weary of a country in which he had met with such terrible misfortunes, and in which all apparently conspired to heighten that superstitious melancholy that had seized upon his mind, he resolved to leave it, and soon arrived at Smyrna. While waiting for a vessel to convey him to Otranto, or to Naples, he occupied himself in arranging those effects he had with him belonging to Lord Ruthven. Amongst other things there was a case containing several weapons of offence, more or less adapted to ensure the death of the victim. There were several daggers and ataghans. Whilst turning them over, and exam-

ining their curious forms, what was his surprise at finding a
sheath apparently ornamented in the same style as the dagger
discovered in the fatal hut—he shuddered—hastening to gain
further proof, he found the weapon, and his horror may be
imagined when he discovered that it fitted, though peculiarly
shaped, the sheath he held in his hand. His eyes seemed to
need no further certainty—they seemed gazing to be bound
to the dagger; yet still he wished to disbelieve; but the particular form, the same varying tints upon the haft and sheath were
alike in splendour on both, and left no room for doubt; there
were also drops of blood on each.

He left Smyrna, and on his way home, at Rome, his first
inquiries were concerning the lady he had attempted to snatch
from Lord Ruthven's seductive arts. Her parents were in distress, their fortune ruined, and she had not been heard of since
the departure of his lordship. Aubrey's mind became almost
broken under so many repeated horrors; he was afraid that
this lady had fallen a victim to the destroyer of Ianthe. He
became morose and silent; and his only occupation consisted
in urging the speed of the postilions, as if he were going to
save the life of some one he held dear. He arrived at Calais; a
breeze, which seemed obedient to his will, soon wafted him
to the English shores; and he hastened to the mansion of his
fathers, and there, for a moment, appeared to lose, in the
embraces and caresses of his sister, all memory of the past.
If she before, by her infantine caresses, had gained his affection, now that the woman began to appear, she was still more
attaching as a companion.

Miss Aubrey had not that winning grace which gains the
gaze and applause of the drawing-room assemblies. There
was none of that light brilliancy which only exists in the
heated atmosphere of a crowded apartment. Her blue eye was
never lit up by the levity of the mind beneath. There was a
melancholy charm about it which did not seem to arise from
misfortune, but from some feeling within, that appeared to
indicate a soul conscious of a brighter realm. Her step was not

that light footing, which strays where'er a butterfly or a colour may attract—it was sedate and pensive. When alone, her face was never brightened by the smile of joy; but when her brother breathed to her his affection, and would in her presence forget those griefs she knew destroyed his rest, who would have exchanged her smile for that of the voluptuary? It seemed as if those eyes,—that face were then playing in the light of their own native sphere. She was yet only eighteen, and had not been presented to the world, it having been thought by her guardians more fit that her presentation should be delayed until her brother's return from the continent, when he might be her protector. It was now, therefore, resolved that the next drawing-room, which was fast approaching, should be the epoch of her entry into the "busy scene." Aubrey would rather have remained in the mansion of his fathers, and fed upon the melancholy which overpowered him. He could not feel interest about the frivolities of fashionable strangers, when his mind had been so torn by the events he had witnessed; but he determined to sacrifice his own comfort to the protection of his sister. They soon arrived in town, and prepared for the next day, which had been announced as a drawing-room.

The crowd was excessive—a drawing-room had not been held for a long time, and all who were anxious to bask in the smile of royalty, hastened thither. Aubrey was there with his sister. While he was standing in a corner by himself, heedless of all around him, engaged in the remembrance that the first time he had seen Lord Ruthven was in that very place—he felt himself suddenly seized by the arm, and a voice he recognized too well, sounded in his ear—"Remember your oath." He had hardly courage to turn, fearful of seeing a spectre that would blast him, when he perceived, at a little distance, the same figure which had attracted his notice on this spot upon his first entry into society. He gazed till his limbs almost refusing to bear their weight, he was obliged to take the arm of a friend, and forcing a passage through the crowd, he threw himself into his carriage, and was driven home. He paced the room with hurried steps, and fixed his hands upon his head, as if he were afraid his thoughts were bursting from his brain. Lord Ruthven again before him—circumstances started up in dreadful array—the dagger—his oath.—He roused himself, he could not believe it possible—the dead rise again!—He thought his imagination had conjured up the image his mind was resting upon. It was impossible that it could be real—he determined, therefore, to go again into society; for though he attempted to ask concerning Lord Ruthven, the name hung upon his lips, and he could not succeed in gaining information. He went a few nights after with his sister to the assembly of a near relation. Leaving her under the protection of a matron, he retired into a recess, and there gave himself up to his own devouring thoughts. Perceiving, at last, that many were leaving, he roused himself, and entering another room, found his sister surrounded by several, apparently in earnest conversation; he attempted to pass and get near her, when one, whom he requested to move, turned round, and revealed to him those features he most abhorred. He sprang forward, seized his sister's arm, and, with hurried step, forced her towards the street: at the door he found himself impeded by the crowd of servants who were waiting for their lords; and while he was engaged in passing them, he again heard that voice whisper close to him—"Remember your oath!"—He did not dare to turn, but, hurrying his sister, soon reached home.

Aubrey became almost distracted. If before his mind had been absorbed by one subject, how much more completely was it engrossed, now that the certainty of the monster's living again pressed upon his thoughts. His sister's attentions were now unheeded, and it was in vain that she intreated him to explain to her what had caused his abrupt conduct. He only uttered a few words, and those terrified her. The more he thought, the more he was bewildered. His oath startled him;— was he then to allow this monster to roam, bearing ruin upon his breath, amidst all he held dear, and not avert its progress? His very sister might have been touched by him. But even if he were to break his oath, and disclose his suspicions, who would believe him? He thought of employing his own hand to free the world from such a wretch; but death, he remembered, had been already mocked. For days he remained in this state; shut up in his room, he saw no one, and ate only when his sister came, who, with eyes streaming with tears, besought him, for her sake, to support nature. At last, no longer capable of bearing stillness and solitude, he left his house, roamed from street to street, anxious to fly that image which haunted him. His dress became neglected, and he wandered, as often exposed to the noon-day sun as to the midnight damps. He was no longer to be recognized; at first he returned with the evening to the house; but at last he laid him down to rest wherever fatigue overtook him. His sister, anxious for his safety, employed people to follow him; but they were soon distanced by him who fled from a pursuer swifter than any—from thought. His conduct, however, suddenly changed. Struck with the idea that he left by his absence the whole of his friends, with a fiend amongst them, of whose presence they were unconscious, he determined to enter again into society, and watch him closely, anxious to forewarn, in spite of his oath, all whom Lord Ruthven approached with intimacy. But when he entered into a room, his haggard and suspicious looks were so striking, his inward shudderings so visible, that his sister was at last obliged to beg of him to abstain from seeking, for her sake, a society which affected him so strongly. When, however, remonstrance proved unavailing, the guardians thought proper to interpose, and, fearing that his mind was becoming alienated, they thought it high time to resume again that trust which had been before imposed upon them by Aubrey's parents.

Desirous of saving him from the injuries and sufferings he had daily encountered in his wanderings, and of preventing him from exposing to the general eye those marks of what they considered folly, they engaged a physician to reside in the house, and take constant care of him. He hardly appeared to notice it, so completely was his mind absorbed by one terrible subject. His incoherence became at last so great, that he was confined to his chamber. There he would often lie for days, incapable of being roused. He had become emaciated, his eyes had attained a glassy lustre;—the only sign of affection and recollection remaining displayed itself upon the entry of his sister; then he would sometimes start, and, seizing her hands, with looks that severely afflicted her, he would desire her not to touch him. "Oh, do not touch him—if your love for me is aught, do not go near him!" When, however, she inquired to whom he referred, his only answer was, "True! true!" and again he sank into a state, whence not even she could rouse him. This lasted many months: gradually, however, as the year was passing, his incoherences became less frequent, and his mind threw off a portion of its gloom, whilst his guardians observed, that several times in the day he would count upon his fingers a definite number, and then smile.

The time had nearly elapsed, when, upon the last day of the year, one of his guardians entering his room, began to converse with his physician upon the melancholy circumstance of Aubrey's being in so awful a situation, when his sister was going next day to be married. Instantly Aubrey's attention was attracted; he asked anxiously to whom. Glad of this mark of returning intellect, of which they feared he had been deprived, they mentioned the name of the Earl of Marsden. Thinking this was a young Earl whom he had met with in society, Aubrey seemed pleased, and astonished them still more by his expressing his intention to be present at the nuptials, and desiring to see his sister. They answered not, but in a few minutes his sister was with him. He was apparently again capable of being affected by the influence of her lovely smile; for he pressed her to his breast, and kissed her cheek, wet with tears, flowing at the thought of her brother's being once more alive to the feelings of affection. He began to speak with all his wonted warmth, and to congratulate her upon her marriage with a person so distinguished for rank and every accomplishment; when he suddenly perceived a locket upon her breast; opening it, what was his surprise at beholding the features of the monster who had so long influenced his life. He seized the portrait in a paroxysm of rage, and trampled it under foot. Upon her asking him why he thus destroyed the resemblance of her future husband, he looked as if he did not understand her—then seizing her hands, and gazing on her with a frantic expression of countenance, he bade her swear that she would never wed this monster, for he—— But he could not advance—it seemed as if that voice again bade him remember his oath—he turned suddenly round, thinking Lord Ruthven was near him but saw no one. In the meantime the guardians and physician, who had heard the whole, and thought this was but a return of his disorder, entered, and forcing him from Miss Aubrey, desired her to leave him. He fell upon his knees to them, he implored, he begged of them to delay but for one day. They, attributing this to the insanity they imagined had taken possession of his mind, endeavoured to pacify him, and retired.

Lord Ruthven had called the morning after the drawing-room, and had been refused with every one else. When he heard of Aubrey's ill health, he readily understood himself to be the cause of it; but when he learned that he was deemed insane, his exultation and pleasure could hardly be concealed from those among whom he had gained this information. He hastened to the house of his former companion, and, by constant attendance, and the pretence of great affection for the brother and interest in his fate, he gradually won the ear of Miss Aubrey. Who could resist his power? His tongue had dangers and toils to recount—could speak of himself as of an individual having no sympathy with any being on the crowded earth, save with her to whom he addressed himself;—could tell how, since he knew her, his existence had begun to seem worthy of preservation, if it were merely that he might listen to her soothing accents;—in fine, he knew so well how to use the serpent's art, or such was the will of fate, that he gained her affections. The title of the elder branch falling at length to him, he obtained an important embassy, which served as an excuse for hastening the marriage, (in spite of her brother's deranged state,) which was to take place the very day before his departure for the continent.

Aubrey, when he was left by the physician and his guardians, attempted to bribe the servants, but in vain. He asked for pen and paper; it was given him; he wrote a letter to his sister, conjuring her, as she valued her own happiness, her own honour, and the honour of those now in the grave, who once held her in their arms as their hope and the hope of their house, to delay but for a few hours that marriage, on which he denounced the most heavy curses. The servants promised they would deliver it; but giving it to the physician, he thought it better not to harass any more the mind of Miss Aubrey by, what he considered, the ravings of a maniac. Night passed on without rest to the busy inmates of the house; and Aubrey heard, with a horror that may more easily be conceived than described, the notes of busy preparation. Morning came, and the sound of carriages broke upon his ear. Aubrey grew almost frantic. The curiosity of the servants at last overcame their vigilance, they gradually stole away, leaving him in the custody of an helpless old woman. He seized the opportunity, with one bound was out of the room, and in a moment found himself in the apartment where all were nearly assembled. Lord Ruthven was the first to perceive him: he immediately approached, and, taking his arm by force, hurried him from the room, speechless with rage. When on the staircase, Lord Ruthven whispered in his ear—"Remember your oath, and know, if not my bride to-day, your sister is dishonoured. Women are frail!" So saying, he pushed him towards his attendants, who, roused by the old woman, had come in search of him. Aubrey could no longer support himself; his rage not finding vent, had broken a blood-vessel, and he was conveyed to bed. This was not mentioned to his sister, who was not present when he entered, as the physician was afraid of agitating her. The marriage was solemnized, and the bride and bridegroom left London.

Aubrey's weakness increased; the effusion of blood produced symptoms of the near approach of death. He desired his sister's guardians might be called, and when the midnight hour had struck, he related composedly what the reader has perused—he died immediately after.

The guardians hastened to protect Miss Aubrey; but when they arrived, it was too late. Lord Ruthven had disappeared, and Aubrey's sister had glutted the thirst of a Vampyre!

THE STORY OF DEMETRIO GKIKAS, THE VAMPIRE OF SANTORINI (1829)

J. Emerson Tennent

Many travel accounts on Greece and the Levant during the late-18th and the early-19th centuries depict the belief in vampires with a mixture of fascination, disgust, and colonialist disdain. They are one of the main sources of the knowledge of the tradition of the vrykolakas in that age. In his Letters from the Aegean (1829), Irish politician James Emerson Tennent (1804-1869) narrates with ardent Philhellenic zeal his journey through the land during the Greek War of Independence. At a certain point, like most of his predecessors, he takes up the recurrent subject of vampirism and, after exhibiting a remarkable familiarity with previous literature, sets out to narrate a recent episode that occurred in Santorini told to him, he says, by a native ship captain. Nevertheless, it is hard to believe that the story was delivered in the form it appears in the book. Given the level of authorial intervention, it is even questionable whether there was a local informant at all. Emerson Tennent presents a romanticized narrative that, far from following the usual schemes and motifs of Greek folkloric accounts, falls under the conventions of contemporary Western fiction in terms of both content and structure. Demetrio Gkikas is a calm and gentlemanly vampire in love lacking the typical vicious abjection of his kind. He excites pity rather than horror. As I suggested earlier in the introduction, this conscious shift from Gothic to romance can be read as an attempt by the Philhellene Emerson Tennent to exorcise the strangeness of the Greek vampire belief and de-orientalize the country by making it sound more familiar to his European audience. The premise underlying the final version of the story is that Greek vampires are of a different, milder sort than the Slavic ones, as befits the rational Hellenic culture they belong to.

THESE traditions are rather antique, but to the present moment the belief is not abandoned in Santorin, and our captain, a steady old man, whom I have before mentioned as a native of the island, informed us of an instance which had occurred to his own knowledge. The father of Demetrio Gkikas, to whom he referred, was a wine-merchant, who lived nigh the plain of Saint Stephen, a district at the south-east of the island, which is remarkable for its fertility, besides being the only landing-place in Santorin at which there is anchorage for ships of burthen.

Demetrio had been brought up to the profession of his father, and till he was sixteen his time had been exclusively devoted to pruning vines, pressing grapes, and tending the subterranean cellar of his father, which was hollowed out of the rocky cliffs nigh the shore; occasionally, too, he had gone in the mystico, which conveyed the Vino Santo and other produce of the island to Syra and Cyprus; but with the exception of these excursions, he had never been beyond the bounds of his native isle, or employed in any other service than the tendance of his paternal vineyards.

His betrothed bride was the daughter of a merchant at Acrotiri; her name was Stefania or Estefania Sessini, and her mother was sister to the father of Demetrio. Their attachment from childhood had been ardent and mutual, and often when the business of the day was done, young Gkika would steal in his shallop along the shore to visit her, or cross off over the hills which separated St. Stephen from the bourg of Acrotiri, to pass the long twilight in wandering round the cliffs with Stefania, or accompanying her songs on the guitar in the garden. In the summer of 1822, she was to complete her fifteenth year, and Demetrio and she were then to be united in the cathedral at Scauro. In the mean time, his father had agreed to divide his vineyard with his son, and the arrangements were to be completed when Demetrio should return from his next voyage to Tenos.

The mystico was laden as usual with wine, and the young merchant set sail with three companions towards the close of February. The weather was cold and stormy, and it was only on the evening of the second day from their departure, that they reached the south of Naxos. Unsuspicious of danger, they held on their course towards Mycone; the night was pitchy dark, and as morning slowly dawned, the unfortunate islanders were thunderstruck to find themselves but a few miles apart from a Turkish squadron, which was sailing with supplies for the Ottoman garrisons in the south of the Morea. Their enemies were too near for them to think of escaping, and the Turks gave them but short time for reflection; a gun was fired athwart their bows, and Demetrio was forced to shorten sail, and await the approach of a corvette which made directly towards them. In the course of a few minutes being found to be Greeks, they were conveyed prisoners on board; the mystico was made fast astern of the Turkish vessel, and all proceeded on their way towards Coron and Navarino.

For the first few months after landing at the former city, Demetrio was employed as a slave by his captors, and occupied from morn till night in working at the fortifications, and toiling in the citadel; but at the end of that period, he was sent along with about fifty others, to be occupied in a similar manner at the fortress of Navarino, which was in hourly expectation of a siege by the victorious Greeks who had already reduced Tripolizza and Malvasia.

Nor was the anticipation unfounded; Prince Ipsylanti, after the fortunate termination of his attempts in the heart of the Morea, despatched Tipaldo, one of his bravest companions, to the assault of Navarino, which was invested in the beginning of June. Notwithstanding the precautions of the Turks, the Greeks had arrived ere the garrison was yet fully supplied with provisions; and the Seraskier, after some brave but ineffectual sallies against the assailants, was forced to retire to the castle, and act solely upon the defensive.

Here, as the approach of famine was every hour becoming more appalling, one of the first measures of the commander was to order the execution of the prisoners, in order to diminish the number of consumers of their now scanty store. Upwards of one hundred were accordingly butchered on the walls in sight of their friends without; some ten or twelve, among whom was Demetrio, saved their lives by abjuring their faith; and one or two alone escaped, by leaping into the *fosse*; and flew to inform Tipaldo of the distress of the garrison, and the apostacy of Gkika and his unfortunate companions.

More politic than brave, the wretched Demetrio had reconciled himself to this degrading alternative, by the reflection that his apparent abjuration was authorized by necessity; that it was merely nominal, as he was still a Christian at heart; and that he could return to the true Church as soon as fortune would consent to favour his escape. But it was contemplated with far other eyes by his bigoted countrymen; and while the Ottomans were doomed to destruction, the renegade Greeks were marked out for *double* vengeance. In the mean time, the blockade was vigilantly observed by Tipaldo; and the devoted Seraskier and his followers prepared with firmness to meet their slowly advancing but inevitable fate.

During this long interval the distracted family of Demetrio awaited in vain his arrival; day after day did Stefania ascend the cliffs of Acrotiri, to watch with wistful eyes the first glimpse of the snowy sail emerging from behind the promontories of Nio, and night after night did she kindle on the steep the wonted fire,

To hail the bark that never must return.

The caiques that had sailed long, long after Demetrio, had all come back from Tinos, but none could bring tidings of the truant boy; while his father fondly hoped, yet feared the hope, that he had only altered his intention, and steered for the more distant port of Syra. But boats soon came from Syra, likewise, and still there were no accounts of his son. Week after week passed on amid mingled fears and hope, but when one month had slowly succeeded to another, and still he came not,

Hope grew to doubt, and doubt soon sickened to despair.

At last the dread intelligence arrived, that he, in whom so many cares were centered, had ceased to be one of his nation and his church; that Demetrio, their adored Demetrio, was an apostate, a renegade, a moslem; leagued with their foes, and marked for slaughter by their friends. The father of Demetrio soon sank beneath the accumulation of shame and sorrow thus heaped at once upon him. He was buried by the chapel of Missaria, and as no Turk was permitted to dwell on or hold property in the island, his farm, the inheritance of his wretched child, devolved upon his distant relatives.

But shame, nor sorrow, nor apostacy, had wrought any change in the breast of Stefania; the dangers of her lover had aroused all the energies of her attachment, and she loved him dearly for the very hatred with which others looked upon his name. In *her* breast, hope had not yet been extinguished; he still lived, and she knew not but that Heaven might yet enable him to return to his unhappy home; and even there, were he to be shunned by all the world, still *her* heart was, like his own, unaltered; and abandoning the rest of mankind, they might fly together to some safe retreat, sacred only to love, and far from the tongue of shame, or the breath of infamy.

But the views of Sessini were far different; and he absolutely started with horror, when he heard his daughter express a hope for the safety of Demetrio, and his speedy return to claim her. "She, Stefania, *his* child, the wife of an Ottoman! No, never: all bonds between them were now dissolved for ever by his apostacy; his name was blasted, his family was dishonoured, his possessions were estranged; henceforth Stefania must learn to forget him." But that was a task more easily enjoined than accomplished; the unhappy girl, however, simulated obedience, whilst her heart was bursting; and yet the smile that sometimes shone upon her lip, was less the effect of effort than the dim sunshine of a distant hope that would still beam across her mind and support her sinking affections.

In the mean time the siege of Navarino was fast drawing to a close: the vigilance of Tipaldo had baffled numerous efforts of the Turks at Coron to throw fresh supplies into the beleaguered city; and day by day the provisions of the soldiery vanished, till at length the last ounce of biscuit was consumed, and the horses of the Seraskier were slaughtered to furnish the mess of the citadel. In turn, every living animal within the walls was killed to supply the cravings of famine; and at length, as a last resource, the papoushes of the soldiers were boiled and gnawed in an agony of famine by the starving but resolute Moslemin. Too weak even to sustain the weight of their sabres, alone, to wield them with their wonted bravery, the gasping soldiers lay stretched in dying struggles around the gates they were left to guard, while their expiring leader sat with his few unbending warriors on the battlements of the castle to await the moment of death.

The Greeks, at this awful crisis, were frantic at once with the intelligence of their recent victories in the Morea, and the news of the slaughter of their Patriarch at Stamboul, and the violation of their churches throughout the kingdom. Tipaldo, wearied with the protracted and inactive siege, prepared for one vengeful and decisive measure. He resolved on making a final and vigorous assault on the walls, whilst he rightly judged that the infidels had no longer energy remaining to defend them. Previously, however, to taking such a step, he despatched a herald to propose to the governor terms of surrender. The Seraskier dismissed the offer with scorn, expressing his resolution to die amidst the walls he could not save; but as the embassy was about to leave the city, some weaker wretches, mad with the pangs of hunger, agreed to listen to the offer of the Greeks, and throw open their gates, on the terms of their lives being spared, and being permitted to retire to Coron. Tipaldo readily complied with their stipulation; and the same evening the city surrendered, and the triumphant Greeks were received within the walls.

Struck with the heroic defence of the Seraskier, the Grecian general treated him with kindness and distinction; his few remaining companions were supplied with food; and during the short period which intervened between the capitulation and the arrival, in the harbour, of some Hydriot vessels, which were to convey the poor emaciated creatures to Modon, each party seemed inclined to observe the items of the treaty. But it was in vain that the apostates attempted to claim a friendly recognition from their conquerors; they were spurned with insult, and told that they must prepare to be despatched to Modon, there to participate in the future fortunes of their adopted friends. Remonstrances, tears, and entreaties, were in vain; and they at length embarked in the Greek vessels along with their fellow-soldiers.

It was sunset when Demetrio went on board, and after a scanty supper, he lay down to rest on the under-deck of the Hydriot. About midnight, however, he was aroused by the noise of hurrying feet and boisterous voices above him, and an instant after a sailor came down to order him on deck.

There he found five others of his companions, who had, along with him, embraced Islamism; they were all that remained from the original number. The Turks were now aroused from their slumbers, plundered of their arms, stripped one by one, and ordered to descend into the boats alongside. Demetrio beheld with terror preparations which he could not well comprehend, but his doubts were all turned to frightful certainty, when he saw the first boat push off from the side, and, gaining a little distance from the ship, the Greeks commenced the work of slaughter. The miserable and defenceless wretches were instantly butchered; the gloom of midnight prevented him witnessing their torments, but he heard distinctly the hewing of the sabres, the crashing of the wounds, the screams of the dying, and the plunges of the mangled bodies, as, one by one, they were flung into the deep. Time after time the murderers returned and carried off fresh victims, till all were destroyed; when the leader of the massacre, approaching the trembling band of renegades, directed them to step into the boat which awaited them.

With screams the devoted wretches besought their infuriated destroyers for mercy, and pleaded but a week, an hour's delay. The Hydriot cast upon them a mingled glance of scorn and pity, and briefly observing, that *death* was a boon too valuable to be conferred on *them*, ordered them instantly to descend over the side; whilst, at the same time, an expressive look reminded the rowers that they knew their duty. Demetrio took his seat in the bloody stern of the boat, which shoved off without delay; he then informed the seaman beside him of his name and family, and offered to reward him handsomely if he would only spare his life; the man returned him no reply, but continued to ply lustily his oar. The boat had now pulled farther from the beach than on any preceding instance, and with straining eyes the wretches within were watching every movement of the seamen, to mark the moment when the work of destruction should begin. The crew, however, rowed on in silence, and they had already gained a mile from the shore, when they headed a little to the right and steered direct for Sphacteria, an uninhabited rock at the mouth of the bay. Here they ran the boat aground, and directing the prisoners to disembark, again put off, leaving them to perish with hunger on the island.

Dreadful as was the alternative, it was still a relief from the sensations of the last half hour, with the instant anticipations of savage murder. Demetrio seated himself on the beach, while his heart felt as if expanding gradually from some unnatural compression; yet still his mind was not at rest; his enemies were still near him, and he felt persuaded they were only gone for a moment, in order to return for the perpetration of some new enormity. He seated himself upon a rock, with his gaze intently bent upon the waters of the bay; and as the first light was dawning in the east, his eyes were gladdened by the sight of the squadron bearing away from the harbour. Still, however, escape was a matter of as great difficulty as before; he was distinctly within view of the town and the fortress, and, as he was now perfectly sensible that he and his companions were landed on the island with the intention that they should perish by hunger, he knew that their movements would be sedulously watched by the garrison.

During the first two days of his exposure, his sufferings were beyond description dreadful. It was the month of August, and not a single tree rose on the deserted isle which might shelter the dying wretches from the scorching sunbeams, and not one drop of water sprung amidst the glowing rocks to quench their ceaseless and intolerable thirst; while all the writhing pangs of gaunt insatiate famine were raging within them. The beach was soon piled with the carcases of their late companions, which came floating in from the shore where they had been flung into the sea; and, as these began to decompose in the heat of the glaring sun, the air grew weighty with the fearful stench. Demetrio bore up courageously under all these accumulated miseries: one by one he saw his comrades fall before him, and at length, on the morning of the third day, he sat upon the hideous rock, the last sad survivor of the immolated garrison.

Weak and almost expiring, hope had not yet totally abandoned him; and he knew, that if he could only gain the opposite shore, which was little more than a mile distant from his prison, he would have no difficulty in reaching the fortress of Modon, and thence effecting his escape to Santorin.

Feeble and emaciated as he was, he fancied that he had still strength remaining sufficient to swim the narrow strait which separated him from the shore. He descended to the beach, and plunging into the waters, found, that though he could not bring a drop of the briny fluid to his lips, his thirst was appeased by the cool immersion of his limbs. It was, however, still too light to attempt the passage of the harbour; he returned to his rock, and having waited till near midnight, he again stripped off his superfluous apparel, and, committing himself to the sea, struck out leisurely towards the distant island. Fatigue soon overcame him, but turning on his back, he lay floating and motionless, till gathering strength enabled him to proceed. Thus, alternately advancing and pausing to recruit his exhausted powers, he continued to proceed by slow degrees, till, some hours ere morning's dawn, he succeeded in reaching the rocky coast.

Fortunately, the spot where he landed was covered profusely with oranges and wild fig-trees, and, securing a quantity of the fruit, he hastened to conceal himself in the clefts of the rocks upon the beach, till coming darkness should favour his flight to Modon.

The news of the surrender of Navarino soon spread over the Cyclades, nor was it long in reaching Santorin; but while all hearts and all tongues were loud and fervent in their joy upon the event of a victory, one bosom alone was burning to know the fate of the conquered. The first report was, of course, that the defenders of the fortress were to be marched out in safety, and Stefania felt half rejoiced; but when the dread intelligence arrived of the exasperation of the Greeks, and the murder of their prisoners, in opposition to the will of Tipaldo, the sound fell like a poisonous blast upon her heart: hope, joy, excitement, energy, all died away within her; the fabric of happiness which her imagination had been long years in raising, crumbled at once to atoms; her bosom grew a desert; and her heart sunk, surrounded, like Marius, only by the ruins of her hopes. Time brought no assuagement of her sorrow, and change no grounds for brighter anticipations of the future. For some months she lingered like a spirit round the haunts of her childhood, restless, joyless, and despairing: at eve, she would be seen reclining by the sea-shore, her eyes fixed upon the wave and her tears falling upon the damp silvery sand; and at morning, as the early fisherman was descending to the strand, he would often find Stefania seated on one of the giant cliffs, with her lustreless eye, pale cheek, and fading form, seeming like a withering flower on the verge of the precipice. Day after day she lingered on in suffering and silence; while her spirits, her beauty, her strength, all, save her memory, were ebbing fast away; and ere that summer was concluded, which was to have witnessed her nuptials, the garlands prepared for her bridal were hung upon her tomb.

But a few days had elapsed from her interment when Demetrio arrived at Santorin. He had succeeded in reaching Modon, had sailed in a Turkish cruiser to Smyrna, and thence returned by Syra and Tenos to his native island. As he stepped on shore at Phira, every eye encountered him with abhorrence; he found that even those on whose friendship he had most firmly calculated shrunk from him with detestation, and the Epitropi, or Elders, suggested in the council a doubt as to the propriety of permitting a Moslem to reside among them. This objection was, however, removed by the first act of the renegade, which was to avow his recantation before the bishop and clergy of the island, and perform a lengthened penance for his temporary estrangement.

But no expiation was sufficient to wash away the impression of his crime from the minds of his countrymen. Shunned, despised, and avoided, he wandered an exile in the land of his birth, where every eye was averted, and every door was closed against him. But still the sorrows of Demetrio did not arise from the privation or persecutions of society, proceeding from a cause which his own heart could not totally condemn; they had a deeper and a cureless origin. A short period might remedy the one; but no extent of time itself could ever restore those whom the grave had torn from him; and the forms of his affectionate father and his adored Stefania were ever haunting his imagination, and adding deeper gloom to his distresses.

"For some time," continued the old man who related the narrative, "he wandered about the shores of St. Stephen and the promontory of Acrotiri, and was occasionally seen in the church of Pyrgos; but he spoke to and associated with none, nor did he even attempt to reclaim from his relatives the estate of his father. For my own part, I always rather pitied than blamed him; and though numbers were of the same feelings with myself, they were deterred, by the fear of his enemies, from showing him either sympathy or kindness. At last, during the winter of 1823, he was missed from his accustomed haunts, and people were the more astonished because his disappearance was at a period when the violence of the weather rendered it impossible for boats to leave the island. The singularity of his departure was spoken of for a time, then all mention of him died away, and at last in a few weeks poor Demetrio was as thoroughly forgotten as if he had never been seen at Santorin. It chanced, however, that one evening, during a tremendous hurricane, which blew over all the Ægean, a boy who had been tending some cotton-plants at the plain of St. Stephen, averred, on his return to Messaria, that he had seen Demetrio seated on a peak of Mount Elias during the storm, and that he had afterwards passed close by him as he was descending the cliff, near the vineyard of old Gkika. For some days the story was laughed at as improbable, but it was soon confirmed by the united testimony of numerous shepherds and fishermen who had met him at various points of the island, and the bay between Acrotiri and St. Nicholas, and to all of whom it was evident that it could be no living being, but a Vroukolakos whom they had encountered. All were convinced that a vampire had taken possession of the body of Gkika; and this very circumstance was sufficient to assure them that his return to Christianity had been acceptable to the Virgin, since no Vroukolakos was ever known to reanimate the remains of a Latin or a Mahometan. Regret for the cruelty with which they had treated him now inspired every mind; and all set out to discover the body of Demetrio, in order to perform an exorcism above it, and procure rest in the grave for his remains. Their search was however in vain, and day after day they returned disappointed from their pursuit, which was at last abandoned.

But the troubled spirit was not yet appeased. Still at midnight and at early morn the figure of Demetrio was seen upon the summit of the bending cliffs that look down upon the bay, and wandering over the hills nigh his former home; but chiefly he was observed to frequent the grave of Stefania, and the spots around the shore where they had so often wandered together by the calm light of evening. Injury he inflicted on none, and so far from disturbing the repose of the villages, he seemed to fly from the walks of the islanders, nor had any individual been able to approach near him, or break in upon his solitary watchings by the shores. One evening, however, a peasant of Acrotiri had seen Demetrio issue from the burial-ground near the village where Stefania was interred. He looked pale and withered, as one must do returning from the grave; he seemed more dead than alive, and he appeared to Georgio scarce able to descend the pass down the cliffs to the sea, to which he betook himself. This narrow path led to a shallow cave under the precipice, into which the caiques of the villagers were drawn up during the inclemency of the winter; and it occurred to the peasant that that spot had not been searched during the pursuit after his remains. The following day he scrambled down the rocks, and entered the cave, and there, as he had anticipated, he found the corpse of poor Demetrio. Like those of all vampires, it was fresh and undecayed,—nay, Georgio said that it was still even warm, and the blood unstiffened; but oh! so pale and emaciated, and wasted away, that it was almost impossible to recognise it. All, even those who had doubted it before, were now satisfied of the fact that Gkika was a Vroukolakos: his remains were conveyed in a boat round the island to the little chapel on Therasia, and an exorcism performed above them. He was then interred at Acrotiri, and when you land you will see his grave beside Stefania's. From that period up to the present, his spirit has returned no more, his memory is no longer detested in Santorin as before, and even those who once censured him for his apostasy, now rather pity his fate and deplore his undeserved misfortunes.

THE VAMPIRE KNIGHT AND HIS CLOUD STEED (1837)

Anonymous

This anonymous story appeared at the end of 1837 in The Keepsake for 1838, a literary annual or gift book whose target audience was largely middle-class young women. Had the piece been published in any other issue of the journal, we would know at this point its author's name. In the 1838 number, though, the editor, Frederic Mansel Reynolds, included an advertisement saying: "The Proprietor having ascertained that a belief exists that the articles for The Keepsake have occasionally been selected less in relation to their intrinsic merits, than to the names of their authors, has determined to escape the imputation, by publishing the work anonymously." Among those names were often popular authors of the day, some of them a central part of the Romantic literary canon such as Mary Shelley, William Wordsworth, or Robert Southey, despite the fact that this kind of publication was not appreciated by critics and lacked prestige.

"The Vampire Knight" is an Orientalist fable set in the 17th-century Ottoman Empire focusing, like many of the sort, on the ethnic and religious struggle between Turks and Greeks in the East. Even though the story shows a decided predilection for the Greeks, it ultimately considers that they belong in the Orient, where their coexistence, even their genetic mixture with "good Turks," is desirable. The vampire is here re-folklorized. Whereas in Polidori's The Vampyre the creature turned from regional demon into a "totalizing monster"—in Franco Moretti's terms—that threatened the whole world, in this story it is presented as a disempowered local superstition. It is however so integrated in the social fabric of these backward, exotic peoples as to become a true force of collective negotiation that can help settle communal conflict.

*Καλίτεροι οἱ ἀδερφοὶ τῆς ἐκκλησίας
παρὰ οἱ ἀδερφοὶ τῆς κοιλίας.*

Brothers of love whom the Church unites,
By solemn prayer, and holy rites,
Are more closely bound, and sincerer far,
Than oft the sons of one mother are.

A BOUT the middle of the seventeenth century, Mustafa
Pasha, a native Turk, was governor of Khaniá. Like the
rest of his correligionists in Crete, he entertained theological notions somewhat lax, and his practice, as will generally
happen, corresponded but too well with the looseness of his
creed. He had married into the distinguished Greek family of
Agriolides, and by the matrimonial contract it was provided
that the wife should exercise freely the rites of her own religion, and, as was often the case, bring up her daughters in
the maternal belief. The sons, if any there should be, were to
follow the faith of their sire. Many, in the oblivion of futurity,
produced by passion, might at first act as unscrupulously as
Mustafa; but few, perhaps, would continue practically to
observe the same toleration when the fever of desire had sub-
sided, and calm reflection had resumed its sway. But he was
by nature gentle and kindly; and, though in theory a genuine
Mussulman, so completely devoid of the prejudices which
usually accompany a belief in the Koran, that he would sometimes, when rising early to prayer, light the taper placed in his
wife's chamber before the panagia.[1] His conduct in this respect
appeared the more extraordinary, in that the lady continued
childless. He took unto himself, however, no other wife, but
continued ever as he had begun, in affection, devotion, gentleness, unchanging and unchangeable.

1 Virgin.

Mustafa's Christian brother-in-law, Demetrio Agriolides, possessed a helpmate who appeared designed by nature to fill up the gap, occasioned by her sister's sterility. In fact, the talent of Madame Agriolides in this matter, was so remarkable, that it acquired her a kind of reputation; so that many a Moslem, with the legal complement of wives, looked upon Demetrio with envy, seeing that his lady filled cradles faster than their entire harems. Every thirteen moons, as sure as the snows melted on the white mountains, Demetrio counted a fresh accession to his family; and beautiful they all were, with their large dark eyes, and Hellenic harmony of features, looking like so many breathing statues from the chisel of Pheidias.

To several of these children Mustafa Pasha, with a stretch of tolerant liberality, not uncommon in Crete, had stood sponsor. He loved children, though childless; and, by a very intelligible sleight of the fancy, was led to imagine that the relation of gossipred opened up between him and his offspring of the font, something like that mysterious channel through which the spirits of affection ascend and descend, like angels over the patriarch's ladder. The soul of Mustafa soared high above the reach of envy; he beheld one lovely infant after another, grace the knees of his friend, and rejoiced to behold them; but when, at last, Theodoros, the youngest and most beautiful of all, whose radiant features lighted up his cradle like a star, was placed on his knees to demand his sponsorship and blessing, it became impossible for him longer to contain his feelings; tears came unbidden to the eyes, and bending down low to conceal them,—"Would to God," cried he inwardly, "that my soul might obtain a boon like this. To become the father of such a son, how gladly would I exchange the Pasha's robes for the mantle of the beggar. Amidst the storms of poverty I would hug him to my bosom; and in sheltering him, in providing for his wants, in stilling his cries, in gathering the honey dew of his smiles, I should be happier than the Padisha. For like a spring in the wilderness is the smile of a child, sweeter is its voice than music, dearer its love than the love of woman. Ah, to embrace thus the son of my soul,—to feel in his touch something purer than light—holier than prayer—more beloved than life. O, Allah! take from me all I possess, so thou but give me, instead, the unspeakable joy of becoming a father."

So prayed Mustafa, nor was his prayer unheard. Two years from that time he found himself at once a parent and a widower. His wife, so tenderly beloved, died in giving birth to a daughter, who, though bright in his eyes as the Pleiades, appeared still no compensation for the loss her coming into the world had caused. Our hearts, in this world, are never without a wound. Nature, when our bliss runs high, provides us with a thorn on which to lean, like the nightingale, that we may remember what we are, and be checked in the fond search after unmingled felicity.

The Pasha, however, was now a father; and, to sweeten the moments of childhood for Emina, obtained from his friend Agriolides permission to shut up along with her in the harem, one of his daughters, a little older than herself. There they grew up together, enjoying such amusements, and pursuing such studies, as suited their age. Emina's beauty meanwhile expanding like the rose-bud, and shedding its light and perfume on everything around, appeared to dazzle and enchant even her female companion, who, during the frequent visits which she paid her friends, dwelt rapturously on her charms, and that incomparable gentleness and softness of character which invests beauty with its greatest power.

As her mother had died so early, Emina was necessarily brought up a Mohammedan, and destined, as a matter of course, to be the wife of some Pasha; for Mustafa entertained in all their plenitude those notions, peculiarly oriental, which regard the marriage and condition of women. He accordingly selected to be the future husband of Emina, his nephew, Youssuf Bey, a young man whose talents and character promised to raise him to the highest offices. Contrary to the customs of the East, he sometimes allowed them to meet and converse in his presence: they were in his eye betrothed. Nevertheless, he could not fail to observe, what, indeed, appeared to be abundantly evident, that, although Youssuf wanted not personal attractions, and enjoyed the reputation of being the best horseman in all Crete, which Mustafa esteemed an important consideration, Emina still met and parted from him with as much coolness as if he had been her aunt. She neither blushed when he approached, nor when, in his absence, allusion chanced to be made to him, did the slightest sigh agitate her fair bosom. In fact, he might have wooed the Sphynx with equal chance of making an impression, as far, at least, as could be conjectured from external signs.

But the Pasha, at that moment, knew nothing of what was passing in his daughter's mind. We have said she was educated a Mohammedan, which, however, only meant that it was taken for granted she believed in the Koran, though no care had been taken to implant such a belief. The presence of Irene Agriolides, in the harem, appeared to have been overlooked; but Emina felt it. They conversed often of religion; and the deep and impassioned enthusiasm of the Christian maiden, her enunciation of mysteries, above their comprehension, but elevating by the very attempt to grasp them, her descriptions, glowing and florid, of the imposing ceremonies,—the incense, the music, the splendour and magnificence of the sacerdotal dress and ornaments, but above all, the secret thrill of devotion which shoots through the heart, when a whole congregation lift up their voices together in praise of their Creator, excited a fascinating power in the imagination of Emina; and if they did not at once convert her, at least awakened a desire to witness the ceremonies of the church.

There would, however, as she foresaw, be some difficulty in gratifying the desire, without demanding of her father a permission he might probably refuse to grant; the youthful friends continued long perplexed and undecided, therefore. To leave the harem accompanied by the usual attendants, slaves or eunuchs, would be to encounter certain detection; to go forth alone they knew to be difficult, and in many ways objectionable. Yet, after earnestly discussing all the reasons, pro and con, this was what they at length determined on. But in an affair of this kind, they found it much easier to resolve than to act. Mustafa's harem, more out of compliance with custom, than from any conviction of its necessity, was most strictly guarded; eunuchs, white and black, beset every door and avenue; female slaves, armed with a graduated authority, from the keeper of my lady's slippers to the keeper of her virtue, occupied the apartments encircling the chamber of Emina; and, therefore, though Irene had always enjoyed the liberty of going forth alone, or attended by a female slave, there seemed to be considerable difficulty in discovering how Emina might smuggle herself out. However, where there's a will, as the vulgar have it, there's a way. It was agreed that one of the female dragons of the harem should be let into the secret, and remain in the sleeping apartment of her mistress, while she, disguised in servile weeds, accompanied her friend, at break of day, to the monastic chapel of Haghios Eleutherios.

The morning fixed upon was Sunday. Irene, who had slept little, rose ere it was light, but found her friend already habited in her masquerade costume, sitting at an open window with eyes riveted upon the dark expanse of the bay below, over which a glimmering gray was imperceptibly creeping from the East. The sound of Irene's well-known footstep put to flight her reverie. "Come," said she, "you see I have long been ready. In my eagerness, at least, I am a better Christian than you. Yet I wish it were well over. God is merciful!"

"There is no ground for apprehension," answered Irene; and led the way towards the street. The approach of dawn is far more rapid in Crete than with us; so that ere they had reached the city gates, the fingers of the mythological Eoos had streaked the sky with purple, violet, and red. A brilliant light filled the atmosphere. From the subjacent sea a breeze, cool and refreshing, came blowing steadily in, communicating buoyancy and vigour to the frame, and lightness to the step;

and though engaged in an act, in her own estimation unlaw-
ful, Emina experienced, from the influence of physical causes,
a kind of mental intoxication, known only to those whose foot
has brushed morning dew from the daisy in the sunny climes
of the East.

The keeper of the gate had too frequently exercised his
office in furtherance of Irene's devotion to hesitate now. They
were, therefore, soon out upon the beautiful plain of Khaniá,
where they immediately struck into the road leading to the
village of Murniés. The scene in itself was by no means new
to Emina. She had a thousand times ridden over it under the
guardianship of her keepers. But the united powers of morning and romance now appeared to invest it with unwonted
magnificence. White and glittering rose the distant villages,
thin, tall minarets, heaven-pointing, and surmounted by gilded
crescents, appearing like columns of snow amid the palm-
trees and cypresses in which they were embosomed. Coveys
of red-legged partridges, disturbed by their footsteps, sprung
whirring from the grass. The sea-mews wheeled in with loud
screams from the bay. While here and there the flight, soaring
and proud, of some solitary eagle, led their eye towards those
giddy heights on which the snows of a thousand winters stood
piled in virgin whiteness.

In less than an hour they passed through Murinés, and
shortly after found themselves near the chapel, whither
they were journeying. It was a building light and graceful,
surmounted by a pillared cupola, and adorned in front with
pilasters in the Doric style, simple cornices, and an angel's
head, supported on wings. The door stood open, and the voice
of singing, such as Emina had never heard, filled the chapel,
and mingled its holy cadences with the morning music of the
brake. They did not immediately enter, Emina's heart failing
her, but stood hesitating among the cypresses that surround
the edifice. When at length, however, they had found courage
to pass the sacred threshold, Emina's eye caught the figure of
a young man who stood with his face towards the minister,

absorbed, apparently, in devotion, and unconscious of the presence around him of any thing save God. His costume, at once rich and simple, bespoke distinction; and his large fair neck, contrasted with the profusion and black curls by which it was partly shaded, suggested an idea of the highest manly beauty, joined with the strength and vigour that enter so largely into the idea women have of it. Irene, who perceived how much she was struck, whispered softly in her ear,—"It is my brother, Theodoros! He will accompany us back to the city, and you shall converse with him."

Emina scarcely heard, for at the moment Theodoros looked round, and his beauty, exceeding that which proverbially belonged to his family, at once kindled up her imagination to a flame. She had never dreamed that human nature could put on a shape so lovely. His face, Hellenic from the outline to the minutest touch of the features, possessed all the ideal dignity of the Apollo, in forehead lofty, in oval roundness of chin as soft as a girl's, and lighted up by large dark eyes hitherto uninspired by passion. But, unused to the world, she forgot that they who gaze are gazed at in return. Theodoros, despite her servile garb, meant partly to conceal her countenance, in a moment discovered the supreme loveliness of a face in which all the distinguishing traits of the Agriolide clan appeared to be concentrated, and carried to the highest perfection. His eye knew not where to rest, on features, or neck, or bosom, or on those rich curvatures into which the youthful female form, when unchecked by fashion, naturally expands. He appeared to be in a dream. A light seemed to radiate from her countenance, and her breath, like a bank of violets, diffused around a delicious perfume, which filled the whole chapel.

The service over, Theodoros hastened to join his sister and demand who and what her companion might be. She at first hesitated to satisfy his curiosity, but being earnestly intreated, was fain to confess the truth; upon which the young man addressed himself to Emina, not in the impetuous language commonly employed by passion in the East, but with timid reverence, such as devotion, in which the heart has share, delights to exhibit. I will not presume to determine on what topics they conversed. The lady certainly forgot the regulations of the harem, listened and replied with earnestness, I might say with warmth, and when near the city gate, they parted, her flushed cheek grew pale, and her feelings experienced that dreary ebb, that chilly stagnation, which in enthusiastic natures inevitably succeed to overwrought excitement. In silence, almost peevish and moody, she stole back to the palace, scarcely noticing the presence of Irene, and was sufficiently fortunate to reach her apartments undiscovered.

The visits to the chapel, thus commenced, became gradually more and more frequent. Emina, converted at once, considered it devotion, Irene supposed it to be love; but was too good a Christian to quarrel with the motive which led her thither, whatever it might be. Devout people, however, are by no means beyond the reach of public animadversion, which, on the contrary, appears to be never so active as when it alights on the back of piety and sheaths its fangs deep in her flesh. The lovers, about whom such mystery floated, were watched narrowly. Emina was traced to the Pasha's palace, Theodoros to that of the Agriolides; and a little drama was quickly invented of which it could not be exactly foreseen whether the denouement would prove tragic or comic.

Some hint of what was going forward at length reached Youssuf Bey, who, in a sullen and revengeful mood, proceeded to the palace, in order to lay the whole matter before the Pasha, and be revenged on Emina because he could not obtain her love. He judged rightly that Mustafa was not a person to be trifled with. It seemed, likewise, quite clear to him, that two opinions could not be entertained respecting the conduct of Emina, which, leading her to associate with infidels, and enter their places of worship, must, he considered, be unquestionably unworthy in every way of a good Mussulman, to say nothing of a Pasha's daughter. Finding the old man sitting alone on his divan, playing with the pipe he had just emptied, he began very gravely by assuring his uncle that something had happened which set all Khaniá laughing at his beard; a feat of wonderful cleverness, seeing it was evident to all the world that as yet he had none. Mustafa inquired very seriously into the nature of his misfortune, but, on learning it, was himself greatly disturbed. He clapped his hands violently, and a slave appearing, commanded Emina to be brought instantly before him. His daughter, of course, obeyed. When she entered the apartment, Youssuf, with a fierce scowl mantling on his face, was standing at her father's side, with one hand grasping his dagger, the other half clenched resting on the back of the couch. His forehead was wrinkled into frowns, his eyebrows had lost their curvature and were uncoiling themselves like dark snakes over his eyes now turned in dudgeon from Emina, his mouth, ruefully drawn down at both sides, looked as if envy itself had shaped it, while the slender moustachios that adorned his upper lip appeared to curl spontaneously, and move like the tail of a cat about to spring upon a mouse. Emina, who in entering, had caught a glimpse of his amiable physiognomy, could scarcely suppress the smile that rose to her lips; but, as her eye descended to her father's countenance, bent upon her with an aspect unusually severe, her levity was checked, and crossing her arms upon her bosom, she humbly inquired his pleasure.

"Who, by the soul of the prophet! am I, Emina, that you dare, without my consent, to quit the harem, and converse openly in the fields with infidels, like one of the female *Yahoodies:*[1] may their faces be black!"

"My lord is angry," replied his daughter, "and as this is new to his slave, she knows not what to say."

"That I am angry is true; but is my anger without cause? Behold my beard! Have not years and sorrows blanched it, my child? Was not my youth buried in your mother's grave, which would have received my wretched frame also, but that for your sake I consented to live? And I considered you a balm

1 Jews.

from Heaven, a charm to dispel my grief, to reconcile me with existence; and now!—but is it true that the daughter of Mustafa Pasha has become the companion of infidels?"

"My lord," answered Emina, "was my mother an infidel?"

"Your mother? She was the chosen of God, my child. What tongue in Khaniá would dare to couple the opprobrious term with her?"

"If not with her, then why with her sister's son and daughter? for with none other have I spoken. Listen to me, my lord. For seventeen years' uninterrupted love and kindness can I ever make you an ungrateful return? Even were you other than my father, your love, burning like an undying beacon over my mother's grave, must long ere now have kindled mine, and knit me to you with links of steel. Do you doubt this, my lord? Wave but one finger in command, and this poniard, in proof, shall be buried in my breast. What have I done? Have I in any thing disobeyed your commands? Was it ever hinted to me that the compact entered into with my mother, now in paradise, would be broken? That the faith of her child should be different from hers? That the religion found good in the wife should be prohibited to the daughter? My lord, I am your slave; but whose is my spirit?"

"Go to, Afrit!" cried the old man, interrupting her, and affecting anger, while the tear trembled in his eye. "Go to; the oil of Roum is on your tongue; you would plead down an ulema. But this comes of instructing women: they will presently, I trow, preach in the mosque, and command in the battle-field."

"Nay, not command," answered she; "but if my lord stood in need of his daughter's arm, he should still find it ready, even on the field of blood."

"Hah! there brake forth the Osmanli. By your mother's soul, Emina, you sport with our beard as the wind with the thistle-down: but, after all, is it true, as we have heard, that you venture to love without our consent?"

"What my lord has heard is true."

"Said I not so?" exclaimed Youssuf, who could restrain his fury no longer. "Said I not so? But the infidel dog"—

"Is my nephew," cried the Pasha, "as you are, Youssuf; but restrain your indignation; we are master in Khaniá, and our daughter shall be slave to no man. There she stands free, to be wooed and won as her mother was. You have my permission to meet and converse with her, even out of my presence, provided, Irene be by: but so has Theodoros; and this shall be for a whole year. At the end of that period she shall become the wife of whomsoever she prefers—and the *only* wife: mark that, Youssuf."

Here the conference terminated. Youssuf retired with a calm and confident brow; but instead of availing himself of the extraordinary indulgence of his uncle, rather shunned than courted occasions of meeting Emina, repaired seldom to the palace, and occasionally absented himself for several weeks together from Khaniá. His father Hassan Zadé, too, the brother of Mustafa, wore an altered mien. From the most supple of courtiers he became suddenly reserved and haughty, and besides entertaining constantly at his house numerous Turks of distinction disaffected towards the Pasha, was suspected of keeping up a secret correspondence with the Porte.

At length this pregnant mystery brought forth. One morning, while Mustafa was sitting in full divan, surrounded by the principal Greeks and Turks of the island, an officer entered with a Hhatti sheriff from Stambool, commanding his immediate attendance at the footstool of the Padishah. To add to his chagrin he was informed, with malicious communicativeness somewhat unusual, that the honours of the pashalik devolved on his brother Hassan. The news, it must be acknowledged, was galling, and altogether unexpected. His indignation was roused: an hour's deliberation allowed him might have severed Crete for ever from the Ottoman empire; but, as in these cases, the bowstring commonly announces the Sultan's displeasure, and there is not a moment to be lost in deciding between obedience and rebellion, the old man was thrown off his guard by the suddenness of the summons, and at once signified his readiness to accompany the officer. It is a maxim of Turkish policy to guard against the danger of insurrection on such occasions by despatch. The same day, therefore, saw Mustafa on the road to Stambool, and Hassan installed in his palace and command.

Emina was not long spared the knowledge of what had befallen. Irene was next day sent home to her parents; eunuchs devoted to Hassan and his son replaced the old servants of Mustafa, and peremptory orders were issued that no one, under pain of death, should presume to quit the precincts of the harem without permission of the Pasha. At the same time Youssuf Bey made his appearance in the female apartments. Haughty and imperious, and desirous less to conciliate than to triumph over his cousin, he commanded her to be brought to him; and in the presence of several witnesses expressed his resolution that their union should take place within a few days: he was not now, he informed her, a humble suitor, the rival of Theodoros, who, it was hinted, had been properly disposed of. Emina, at this stage of the proceedings, turned pale as ashes, and seemed fearfully agitated; but uttered not a word. It was judged proper, however, to remove her; she was therefore led back to her chamber and placed under the care of a young female slave, her milk-sister,[1] a relative not less closely bound by affection, in the moral theory of eastern nations, than a sister by blood.

Left alone together, they at first gave vent to their sorrows in sighs and tears: but these mend nothing. Something more than weeping would be necessary to defeat the machinations of Youssuf and his father; and after long deliberation, a scheme was hit upon which appeared likely to be attended with success. As the Turks regard insanity with the most superstitious reverence, not unmingled with terror, supposing it to be always under the especial protection of Heaven, it was agreed that Emina should feign madness, and utter, in its

[1] The oriental expression.

furious paroxysms, many wild and fantastic things, foaming, meanwhile, at the mouth, rolling about her eyes, and doing frantic violence to herself and others. Accordingly, at the dead of night, Kamerilza, for that was the name of the slave, burst forth with loud cries from their chamber, pursued by Emina, who, with a lamp in one hand and a toasting-fork in the other, kept up a fierce chase along the corridors, exclaiming that she had discovered a *Katakhanas* (vampire) in her bed. The whole palace thrown into confusion by this device, believed every thing they saw to be real; and it was the general opinion that the curse of God had fallen on the place to avenge the ruin of Mustafa, whose absence was deeply deplored. Even Youssuf and his father, whose wickedness afforded them no protection against superstition, though at first some doubts crossed their minds, soon fell into the general belief. Observing which, for they suffered many proofs of their conviction to escape them, Emina redoubled her manifestations of madness; and so ably did she act her part, that Kamerilza more than once experienced the suspicion that her mistress had passed from jest to earnest.

In the meantime a report of their proceedings was diligently conveyed to Theodoros, who, with his spiritual brother, had prudently retired from the city and taken refuge with the monks of Haghios Eleutherios. The nature of the brotherhood, in Crete called Spiritual, is this:—Two young men, desiring to render eternal the ties of friendship that bind them to each other, repair to the church, and there, in the presence of God, with solemn rites and a service set apart for that purpose, declare themselves brethren, and contract voluntarily, and vow to perform, all the obligations imposed by that relationship. To these young men, I say, Kamerilza contrived to furnish daily an exact account of what took place in the palace. It was foreseen that neither the strength nor arts of Emina could long hold out. She must certainly sink under the efforts requisite to support the part she had undertaken, or might, in an unguarded moment, betray herself. They resolved, therefore, at all hazards, to attempt her deliverance; but it was exceedingly difficult to discover what course they should pursue, having at once to contend with power, and the watchful vigilance of vindictive jealousy.

Love, however, is fertile in expedients. Familiar from their boyhood with the superstitions of their native land, they knew that, in the mountains above the convent where they now lay hid, a spectre was said periodically to appear, to which the Sfakian peasants had given the appellation of the "Vampire Knight and his Cloud Steed." Of this equestrian phantom, people of all ranks in that part of the island stood in awe. He was said to have been a wicked Venetian governor who, some centuries ago, had committed unheard of crimes, and died excommunicated; on which account his spirit had been condemned to roam the earth as a Katakhanas, or vampire, till the day of judgment. His horse, by some accident, had been converted, like himself, into a spectre; and mounted on his back, the Knight would, from time to time, flit like a mist across the mountains, inspiring dread into the peasantry, and giving rise to the belief that disasters and calamities were about to fall upon the country. Had the spot where he was buried been known, they might have opened his tomb, and burned the body, which would immediately have put him to flight; but time having thrown its mantle over this circumstance, nothing remained but to endure the visitation when it came.

Theodoros secretly purchased a white horse of great strength and beauty, mounted upon which, attired in the old Venetian costume, he nightly made his appearance aloft on the summits of the cliffs, now glancing rapidly along in the moonlight, and now plunging into the thick of the pine forests. The report that the Vampire Knight was come again spread like lightning. For many miles round every man trembled in his bed, doubled the number of his prayers, and crossed himself diligently on the approach of nightfall. Not a bright cloud rested on the mountain peaks, but superstition converted it into the Knight. Not a lightning flash shot across the sky, but

it was said to be the gleam of his spear. No man died, but the
Vampire Knight was thought to have supped upon his liver.
The imagination of the whole neighbourhood was in fact
turned topsy-turvy, and their eyes, as too commonly happens,
did willing service to that inventive faculty; so that, as often
as Theodoros was beheld traversing the mouth of some glen,
standing in a broad gap among the crags, his figure relieved
against the deep blue sky, or galloping rapidly across any of
the small table-lands among the mountains, it was confidently
affirmed that flames issued from the earth, while thunders
rolled above, and hurricanes roared and rent themselves away
through the forests.

Meantime things were growing worse and worse in the
palace, where Emina's ravings became at length so terrific, that
a suspicion more than once crossed the minds of Hassan and
his son Youssuf that she herself was not better than a vampire.
They, however, resolved to leave no stone unturned in search
of a remedy for her malady. Every old woman in Khaniá, who
pretended to be cunning, was called in and consulted; every
vender of drugs or charms enjoyed an opportunity of trying
the force of his wares on the person of Emina, and verses of
the Koran, written on the skin of an unyeaned lamb,—some
say, on that of a child prematurely born,—were suspended
in such profusion round her neck, that, when armed with all
her spells, she looked exactly like an itinerant poulterer in the
streets of Stambool on a windy day, with a whole flight of
small-fowl dangling round his neck.

At length a wandering Derwish, with a triangular harp upon
his back, a beard of portentous dimensions, a Toorkoman kerchief twisted about his head, and a most ample *khirkheh*, or
religious habit, bound with a broad girdle about his loins, was
observed walking slowly in front of the palace, crying aloud,
"Who will buy my spells? I am the Derwish Isfendiah from
the holy city of Medina. I can cure the lame, give speech to
the dumb, and make the man with one eye see clearer than he
who has two. Who will buy? Who will buy?"

Kamerilza, who happened to be at the window of a turret in the harem, ran down speedily to inform the Pasha of the jewel of a Derwish whom the prophet had, as it were, thrown into their mouths. "Perhaps," said she, "his skill may even reach the disease of the Lady Emina. Who knows? Shall I call him in?"

"You may call him," replied the Pasha; "and, meanwhile, we will ourselves pay her a visit. The presence of so holy a man can do us no harm."

The faithful slave would very gladly have dispensed with the honour his Highness was about to do her mistress, for as often as he made his appearance her raving became more frightful than ever. But what was to be done? Without farther parleying with herself, she ran after the Derwish, and, "Holy man!" said she, "have you any spells for madness?"

"Child," replied he, "it is the universal epidemic. To what purpose, therefore, should I travel, did I not number among the secrets of my art the power to expel the demon which is the cause of what you term madness. Is there any one in His Highness' household afflicted by that spawn of Gehennan?"

"If you will follow me," rejoined Kamerilza, "you shall judge."

She accordingly led the way, and the Derwish walked after, crossing several courts and corridors, until they at length arrived at the door of the apartment where Emina lay reclined upon a couch, at the foot of which stood her uncle Hassan. Her countenance was greatly altered from what it had been. At one moment her eyes rolled fearfully, her lips quivered, the colour forsook her cheeks, and her dark streaming hair rose and fell upon her beating bosom, or was thrown wildly back upon her shoulders. Then a calm would ensue, and she would look intently upon the bare wall, play carelessly with the jewelled rings upon her fingers, or snatch up some instrument of music, and run confusedly over its strings. The old Pasha grasping his left elbow with one hand, and thrusting the other into his beard, stood looking on with an envious savage scowl. He seemed to regret that so fine a specimen of humanity should not be instrumental in giving future Pashas to Khaniá. Otherwise, his predominant feeling might be said to be one of triumph. If Youssuf could not have her, so neither, thought he, could Theodoros. And there was some comfort in that.

Kamerilza had already entered, and was beginning to describe to the Derwish the exact condition of her mistress' mind, ere the Pasha appeared aware of their presence.

"Ah, Derwish," cried he, as soon as his eye caught the old man's figure, "you are welcome. The Prophet, we hear, hath blessed you with the skill to subdue diseases; and should you, in this case, exercise that skill successfully, you will not find us ungrateful."

"God is God," replied the Derwish, "and all things are in his hands. Whatever poor skill I possess shall be at the service of the lady; and if Providence so wills it, I will deliver her. But how?" exclaimed he, wildly looking about. "Why, where is the lad that attended me?"

"I saw no lad," answered Kamerilza.

"Ah! yet my box of spells are in his hands. Go, Khatoon, call him hither. You will find—But stay," said he, "have you got a single feather of the white ibis in the palace?"

"Such," inquired the Pasha, "as are used in amulets?"

"The same," replied the Derwish.

"I think," muttered Hassan, musing, "there may be such a thing in my private treasury."

"Oh, if that be the case," cried the holy man, with a look of great confidence, "there will be no cause to despair. It is the only thing wanting to complete my spell; for I have the feather of the *rokh*, of the *rakhama*, of the *almazir*, of the *semenda*, and the *anka megareb*. Be thankful to the Prophet, Pasha, for the thing is done."

"Say you so, holy man?" exclaimed Hassan, "then I will fetch it myself."

With these words he quitted the chamber, and Kamerilza ran forth in search of the Derwish's attendant, leaving him alone with Emina.

"Now, lady," said he, "is the moment for escape. Irene will be presently here. She will change dresses with you, and take your place. You must fly with me. Theodoros awaits you near the monastery. Every thing is in readiness—horses, attendants, arms. I am his spiritual brother; and to remove all doubt, have brought the ring from his finger to place in your hands."

Before Emina could recover from her astonishment, Kamerilza returned with Irene, in the garb of a boy; and, in the midst of suppressed greetings and half-muttered fears, the exchange of outer garments was effected. The youthful Greek then reclined on the couch, and her friend, disguised as a poor lad, fell back to a remote part of the chamber, as if from respect for the holy man, and, with tremulous hands, grasped the box of amulets and spells. The Derwish then seized his harp, and it was agreed, that, as he played, the patient should grow still, and feign to be asleep. He would then place the spell on her breast, pronounce his benediction, and promise to return on the morrow.

Ere their arrangements, however, had been well completed,—for it had been proposed to provide for Irene's escape likewise—the sound of the Pasha's footsteps was heard in the passage. Upon this, the new actor began to moan aloud, and twisting and tearing her hair, which she had purposely let fall over her face, now and then set up a loud shriek. The Derwish, as if in a dream, struck loudly the chords of his harp, chanting, at the same time, a plaintive mystical air, such as the Persian soofis, when smitten with love, sing over their wine goblets. He took care that the words he uttered should have no meaning at all, knowing well that mankind are most apt to reverence what they do not comprehend. Hassan, who, on entering, observed the Derwish, with uplifted eyes, playing earnestly on his harp, the boy huddled up with his box, strings of holy beads, parchment amulets, and other sacred things, half behind the door, Kamerilza with one finger on her lips and eyes fixed upon the supposed Emina, who groaned deeply, and threw her form into a slow undulating motion, was stricken with a kind of awe, and stood still, holding the precious feather of the white ibis in his hand.

"She will sleep presently," whispered the Derwish.

"Inshallah,—please God,"—muttered Hassan.

Accordingly, when beginning to grow tired of her exertions, Irene became gradually tranquil, and edged herself down upon the couch, until the shawl which Kamerilza had thrown over her, partly covered her averted face. She then appeared fast asleep, and the Derwish, cautiously lowering his music, suffered it at length to die imperceptibly away. He then received the magical feather from the hand of the Pasha, and binding it up along with several others, supposed to have been plucked from birds that appear only once in a thousand years, sprinkled over them a certain red liquor which he carried about with him in a phial, and then lightly laid the spell upon the breast of the sleeper. Both the Pasha and the Derwish then retired from the apartment, leaving Kamerilza to watch over her mistress. The holy man, on quitting the palace, refused the reward proffered him, observing, that he wished to do good for the love of God; and, promising to return on the morrow, issued, along with Emina, into the streets, and was soon lost in the narrow intricate courts and alleys abounding in every part of Khaniá.

By a particular stroke of misfortune, Youssuf Bey, who had been out hunting all the morning, returned some time before dark; and, on being informed of what had happened, insisted upon seeing Emina. His father, after at first seeking to dissuade him, yielded at length to his importunities. They proceeded together, therefore, to the harem, and approaching on tip-toe, supposing she might be still asleep, heard Irene discoursing very rationally with Kamerilza. Youssuf's rage knew no bounds. He sprang like a lion into the chamber, and perceiving the beautiful Greek in the place and habit of his intended bride, would certainly have poniarded her on the spot, had it not been for the prompt interference of his father. Thrown suddenly off her guard, and supposing the lovers beyond pursuit, Irene, in a burst of passion, defied their vengeance; informed them, that Emina was by that time safe under the protection of her brother; that they would fly to the mountains, and there, surrounded by the bold Sfakians, set at nought their malice and their power.

Youssuf heard no more. Rushing forth into the court, he commanded his horse, always ready saddled, to be instantly brought forth, and a number of horsemen to attend him. His suspicions, directed by the former visits of Emina to that church, immediately pointed towards Murniés and Haghios Eleutherios. As soon, therefore, as he and his followers were in the saddle, the whole band dashed forth, and galloping furiously through the streets, overturning sundry asses and paniers in their career, had speedily passed the city gates and reached the skirts of the plain, on which, at no great distance, the Derwish and Emina were moving along at a brisk pace. Though scarcely expecting to be so quickly pursued, the Derwish, ever on the watch, presently perceived the horsemen in their rear. He therefore glided with his charge into a grove of wild olive trees, and following narrow footpaths, well known to him, still proceeded in the direction of the monastery, near which Theodoros, with a number of friends and dependents, was to receive Emina from his hands.

The day was now far spent, and thick shadows, cast partly from the mountains, fell upon the track both of pursuers and pursued. Emina's heart sickened within her. They were still at no great distance from the road, which, through openings in the trees, they could command a view of, when the troop of horsemen, enveloped in clouds of dust, swept by. From the rapidity of their movements, they were soon far ahead, so that by taking a different track, they might easily, for the present, have effected their own escape; but, as to join Theodoros formed their sole object, it was necessary to proceed, even in the footsteps, as it were, of those whom they would most have shunned. They could distinctly hear the clatter of their steeds' hoofs until they came suddenly to a halt at the gate of the monastery. The fugitives, still moving through the woods, and avoiding the village, made a circuit to the right, and at length reached a small eminence overlooking the sacred edifice, of which the moon, now shining brightly on the scene, enabled them to command a complete view.

Youssuf, in a loud and angry tone, had several times commanded the monks to appear and unbolt the gates, threatening to break them in case of refusal. The good fathers, too well versed in the history of Turkish violence, sat trembling in their cells, fearing equally to obey and disobey. Resistance they knew to be vain. For how could they withstand the power of the Pasha? Yet, if they admitted the furious miscreants, who could answer that their blood would not be shed, even before they knew wherein they had offended?

The hour now approached in which Theodoros expected the arrival of his spiritual brother, with Emina. Every moment the deep anxiety of his mind augmented, as he beheld the moon rising higher and higher in the firmament, lighting up the summits of the mountains, and shedding a bright radiance over the streams. He listened tremblingly to every breeze which ruffled the foliage of the tall cypresses, and as the owl hooted in the ivied cliffs, or the wild dog's bark came reverberating down the heights, started wildly in his saddle, as if smitten by an arrow. As the minutes proceeded without bringing the object of his love, his impatience rose almost to agony; and, contrary to the advice of his friends, he quitted the spot where it had been fixed they should meet, and rode down the tortuous rocky path leading to the monastery. From time to time, as he descended, it seemed as if loud voices smote upon his ear. To these, at no long interval, a crash succeeded; and presently, a deep red glare filled the court of the building, which a short time convinced him was in several places on fire.

Theodoros could now restrain himself no longer. He imagined that some accident had driven Emina to take refuge there, and concluded that she had been pursued, and that the monks, refusing to give her up, were now suffering the vengeance of the Turks. He was accompanied by fifteen young men, mounted like himself, and armed to the teeth. He instantly imparted his suspicions to them; and, receiving their renewed promise to stand by him in all extremities, he gave his Cloud Steed the spur, and a few minutes saw him in front of the burning monastery. The Turks, not fewer than twenty in number, who had many of them alighted from their horses, were enjoying the conflagration they had created; and Youssuf, having ransacked the whole building in search of Emina, was himself among these. But, when the shout of the Greeks, and the loud trampling of their horses' hoofs, were heard without, he speedily rushed forth, and vaulted like a thing of air into his saddle. The cry at the same moment, arose of "The Vampire Knight! the Vampire Knight!" and Theodoros, mounted on his milk-white barb, emerged from among the cypresses, and stood like a spectre in the full glare of the conflagration. With a rush, he might at that moment have stricken down the bravest of his enemies. They sat aghast on their horses, or stood motionless beside them, with foot lifted towards the stirrup, mouth half open with wonder, and eyes round and glaring like fire-balls. His appearance was doubtless sufficient, in that superstitious land, to justify their terror. Armed cap-a-pié in white, with helm and nodding crest of the same colour, bearing a long white spear in his hand, and mounted on a fiery horse, that seemed to have been hewn out of Parian marble, or shaped of morning mist, few that saw him would have been able wholly to repress a feeling of apprehension. But he had, nevertheless, forfeited by this movement much of the advantage he hoped to derive from putting on the form of the Vampire Knight. Men quickly grow familiar with their fears. That which does not destroy is despised; or, at least, reduced to the plain level of humanity.

But Theodoros, content to rely on his valour alone, had no sooner reconnoitred his foes, and distinguished among them the form of Youssuf Bey, than giving the signal to his friends, he commenced the attack, spearing more than one, unhorsing several, and making clear way in whatever direction he turned his steed. Youssuf, however, though naturally brave, appeared reluctant to encounter him. While every other Greek and Turk rushed upon each other, while pistols were fired, sabres drawn and horse urged against horse, he wheeled about on the green, giving his orders, but shunning Theodoros, and keeping his sword unfleshed. At length, however, to avoid him became impossible. His fierce foe seemed to seek him alone; and, directly in front of the great gate, they met. Youssuf, seeing his antagonist armed with a long spear, like a Bedouin, which with his sabre he should be unable to parry, drew his pistols and fired both, but, had the mortification to perceive, without effect. Theodoros then rushed upon him; and while, by a sudden movement, he sought to turn aside, the spear entered his horse's flank, and brought both steed and rider to the ground.

The spectacle now offered by the monastic lawn, wont at other times to be so calm and peaceful, was full of strange terror and confusion. From the burning monastery, chiefly of wood, the flames ascended crackling, hissing, and spitting to the clouds, while an intense heat filled the air, and a dark red glare fell upon the cypresses and other trees, and on the figures of the combatants, some struggling on horseback, others rolling in blood upon the green sward. In the building itself not a sound was heard but that of the flames, no shrieks, no loud lamentations. The Greeks concluded that every monk had perished by the sword, and Emina, together with her holy protectors. Before driving his lifted spear through the heart of Youssuf, Theodoros, therefore, in a loud voice demanded of him an explanation:

"Hast thou slain her, accursed infidel?" cried he. "Say, son of a dog, say she has not, with my spiritual brother, fallen a victim to thy rage, and I may spare thee even now."

"Nay," cried Youssuf, striving to free himself from the stirrups and gain his feet, "nay, it is thou who hast slain her, if she be slain. But, spare me not! I will not ask thee for life, thou son of a burnt father!"

And, with a violent effort, he freed himself from his dying horse, and leaping back a pace or two, stood with drawn sabre before Theodoros, who paused to strike him thus at disadvantage. While they remained in this position, a piercing shriek was heard in the grove on the east of the lawn. The combatants, with one consent, ceased from strife for a moment, while the figure of a Derwish, followed by a woman, came rushing across the green. Excepting Theodoros himself, none, whether among the Turks or among the Greeks, could conjecture what this extraordinary apparition might signify. In another moment, however, their doubts were cleared up. Urging forward his horse with a bound, Theodoros snatched her from the earth, and calling aloud that Emina was found, and bidding his companions follow, turned the face of his Cloud Steed up the steep of the mountain, at the heels of the fleet-footed Derwish; and, in a few minutes, every surviving Greek had disappeared among the trees.

This movement had been executed so rapidly, that Youssuf Bey was unable even to attempt a rescue. As several of his companios, however, had fallen, he easily found a horse without diminishing his force; and, mounting rapidly, pursued the enemy's track, which he was enabled to discover from the noise their horses made in galloping. But, though his companions obeyed his commands, he perceived they were by no means anxious to overtake the Vampire Knight. It was in vain that he protested it was no other than Theodoros Agriolides. They made no reply; but did not, therefore, the less doubt what he affirmed; and, in fact, several of them were afterwards ready to make oath that they saw the moon through the spectral steed, which more than once, they said, during the contest, was heard to converse with its master in Italian. After toiling up the heights for some time to no purpose Youssuf relinquished the pursuit therefore; and cursing the beard of Theodoros and every other Greek, returned towards the city. On the way, the unmanly resolution grew up in his mind to wreak his vengeance on Irene, who, at all events, he thought was in his power. This afforded him some consolation. He, accordingly, quickened his pace, and soon reached the palace; but, on arriving, had the mortification to find that both Kamerilza and his intended victim had disappeared during the confusion of the afternoon; so that nothing now remained but to pour forth his rage upon the Greek nation in general, and the Agriolides in particular.

Theodoros and Emina reached the Sfakian mountains in safety, where they were immediately united, according to the solemn rites of the Greek Church. He then, through the medium of his spiritual brother, who could put on as many different shapes as Proteus, opened communications with his family, who lived on terms of friendship with many of the principal Turks of Khaniá. Representations were secretly dispatched to the Porte. The misstatements and fabrications of Hassan Pacha and his son were demolished, partly by evidence, partly by that argument which is irresistible in all courts,—I mean a syllogism in the shape of sequins,—and one fine morning, when no one looked for any thing so fortunate, the beloved countenance of Mustafa Pasha was again beheld in the streets of Khaniá. Great were the rejoicings of the people, both Turks and Greeks. The city rose like one man to receive their favourite Governor. Thousands of youths, with burnished arms, and faces of gladness, accompanied him to the palace, where the Hhati Sheriff of the Sultan quietly reinstated Mustafa; while Hassan and his son, at the command of their sovereign, sank back reluctantly into the obscurity of private life. Not many days afterwards, Theodoros and Emine were at the Pasha's side, and the old man had, in due process of time, the satisfaction of seeing a beautiful young family striking root about him.

In gratitude to the monks of Haghios Eleutherios, who had escaped by concealing themselves in an artificial cavern, scooped beneath their garden, the Agriolide family rebuilt the monastery and chapel upon a larger scale than before; and thither the fair Emina ever after repaired to exercise her devotions. Irene united to the honest Derwish, was still her companion; and the Vampire Knight, the happiest of men, and the fondest of husbands, is still, in his twofold capacity of Devil and Lover, celebrated throughout all the Western parts of Crete.

VAMPIRES (1839)

John Bowring

The life of John Bowring (1792-1872) was strikingly eventful. A politician, merchant, linguist, translator, writer, diplomat, political industrialist, and Member of Parliament at different stages, he was appointed Governor of Hong Kong in 1854, remaining in office till 1859. Though not a Philhellene in the conventional sense of the term, he was instrumental in the creation of the London Greek Committee in 1823. In fact, his was the idea to raise a loan in aid of the struggling Greeks. A few years later, however, he was accused of deceiving investors and mismanaging the funds, and his name remained connected with the so-called "Greek Pie" scandal for the rest of his life. Among his many literary and scholarly works is Minor Morals for Young People, *published in three volumes between 1834 and 1839. In the third volume is a chapter on Greek vampires that denotes a certain knowledge of Balkan and Eastern lore, though it is not certain whether he ever visited Greece. In any case, this volume was clearly influenced by his 1837-38 visit to Egypt, where he came into contact with the burning Eastern Question (the internal conflicts within the declining Ottoman Empire that threatened to lead to its dismembering, a matter which deeply concerned Britain and France in their aspiration to keep Russian expansion at bay). Considering his recent experience and his understandable personal resentment with Greek affairs, it is no wonder that Bowring presents the Greeks in an entirely Oriental frame, subject to Turkish authorities and utterly disenfranchised. It would not be exaggerated to say that Bowring's piece works in exactly the opposite direction from Emerson's: re-Orientalizing Greece by depicting its traditions in Orientalist fashion as part of the East. Here, the vampire is once more de-gothicised and re-folklorized. In addition, the concluding remark of the narra-*

tor after a perspicacious comment by the children connects the social dimension of the superstition to the Greeks' inherent deceitfulness.

On a different note, it is worth noting that Bowring's book includes an engraving showing the vampire in his lair which is the only known graphic representation of the vrykolakas *before the 20th century.*

"WHEN will you tell us, Papa! some more stories about Fairies or Ghosts, for a little variety, you know, is so pleasing?" said Edith to Mr Howard, as the time for their evening conversation approached.

"Why, we will take the opinion of the majority, Edith!" replied her father. "What says Mamma?"

"O Mamma!" exclaimed one of the boys; "I am sure Mamma will let us support Edith's motion to-day, and Papa will give us something supernatural."

"So be it, children!" said Mrs Howard, consentingly, "and we will be unanimous in our petitions to Papa."

"Agreed!" responded Mr Howard; "and I think I will give you some account of the Vampires, of which I dare to say you have often heard. And no Oriental superstition is more general or more disgusting than the belief in *Chadés*, or Vampires. A dead body will become a Vampire, it is said—if, for the first week after death, it is exposed to the action of the sun's rays; and, if forty days are allowed to pass without the removal of the corpse from such a situation, it is no longer to be found among the dead, but receives its horrible mission to torment and to alarm the living.

"Some of the proceedings of the Vampires are more mischievous than wicked. They pour vinegar into wine, mix honey and meal together, salt with sugar, oil with butter; but they also beat, and sometimes are said to murder, their old acquaintances. They appear either in the character they had while alive, or assume the shape of an animal, or even wander about invisible upon the earth.

"So little doubt attaches to the existence of Vampires that

the Cadi of a district is frequently applied to for an Ihlam, or authority, to enable a *Chadedgi* or *Vampirdgi* (Vampire-hunter) to visit burial-places, to examine graves, and to take any other measures to discover and to defeat the machinations of Vampires. These men profess to be gifted, by means of certain herbs, with the power of tracking a Vampire even when he is invisible to others. They act gratuitously, refusing all recompense; but are bound not to communicate their unknown secrets to any but their hereditary descendants. The opinion generally maintained is, that the Chadedgi are themselves descended from Vampires on the paternal side; and it is an undoubted fact that, in the districts where the Vampires are most common, the Vampirdgis are to be found in the greatest numbers. The remedy grows with the growth of the evil.

"Having obtained, then, authority from the Cadi, the Vampirdgi sets out on a visit to all the tombs in the neighbourhood, and sometimes undertakes a journey of many leagues. He discovers, by arts unknown, the tomb of the Vampire; and on the following Saturday (for it is only on Saturday that the Vampires are *at home*) the Vampirdgi, the local authorities, and crowds of people hasten to the place, which is surrounded by men on horseback, each with a drawn sabre in his hand. Nobody can tell why there are so many guards—but so it is; and, under the direction of the Vampirdgi, the grave is opened, and the body is always discovered—the skin peeled off, the muscles fresh and red but swelled, the hair and beard (if it be the corpse of a man) considerably lengthened. There is no disagreeable odour, but the smell is solely that of newly-uncovered earth. (Remember, this is the account given by the people themselves). The spectators all retire to some distance, while the Chadedgi drives a pointed stake through the heart of the corpse, from whence there is always an emission of blood. The crowd then approach, a funeral pile is prepared, and the body, with the stake, is burnt till they are both wholly consumed—and, the ashes being deposited in the grave, the Vampire can molest his neighbours no more. The proceedings vary somewhat in different parts of the East; those I have described are exactly such as take place in the Turkish provinces of the Danube.

"It is not an uncommon thing for a Governor, at the request of a district, to order the burial-place to be changed, when it is suspected of being favourable to the creation of Vampires. Old Ali Pacha of Jannina issued several such decrees; and I have known instances where the inhabitants of whole villages have left their houses and passed the night in the fields, when it was supposed a Vampire had got into their habitations.

"At Seres, in Macedonia, there was a Vampire which created great disturbance. He often visited the house in which he had dwelt when alive, and amused himself by pelting the persons he found in it with pigeon's dung. One day, when there was a large company, a daring young man bid defiance to the Vampire, told him to show himself, and challenged him to single combat. He was answered by a shower of pigeon's dung— upon which he drew a pistol from his belt, and fired at the spot whence the shower proceeded; but great was everybody's astonishment when, instead of going directly to the object, the ball stopped in the middle of the room and fell perpendicularly down upon the floor. Immediately quantities of dirt were hurled at the persons who were present, and they were obliged to fly from the place.

"A Vampirdgi was immediately sent for, and he came, accompanied by a crowd of people. Placing himself in the middle of the court, he wrote an inscription on a piece of paper, which he threw into the air, where it continued describing circles for more than a quarter of an hour, when it fell perpendicularly to the ground. The Chadedgi immediately drove a staff, with a sharp iron point, through the paper—and, on lifting it up, a small frog was seen pierced through by the iron. A fire had been before kindled, and in the midst of the fire he placed the staff, the paper, and the frog—and, when all were consumed, the ashes were collected, taken to the churchyard, and buried; and the village was never afterwards disturbed by the Vampire.

"A district celebrated for its number of Vampires is that of Sari-gueul, in the neighbourhood of Salonica. Any one who likes to visit that part of Macedonia might fill a volume with the stories he could collect. That which I am about to relate was related by the Governor, and verified by the Mufti, of Vodéna, who said that fifteen hundred persons were willing to swear to the truth of the statement.

"In the village of Emboré there died, some years ago, a Greek peasant of the name of Marco Loutche. He left a widow and two daughters, aged eight and ten years. One evening, about three months after his death, while the woman and her children were employed in spinning flax by lamp-light, Marco appeared. The door had not been opened, and they were naturally alarmed by the presence of a man, whom they at first supposed to be a robber; but their alarm was increased tenfold when they perceived that their visitor was one of the dead—that he was her husband and their father. But he spoke to them in gentle tones—declared he would do them no harm—that his visit was one of affection—and that, with their consent, he proposed to pass every night in their company. He said that he should not come empty-handed in future; and, in fact, at his next visit, he brought them each a pair of loose trowsers, such as are worn by Oriental women. Every evening something was added to their wardrobe, or to their stock of culinary ware and household furniture; while in the village of Emboré, and the neighbouring villages, nothing was heard of but the robberies of garments, chairs, tables, pots and pans—and nobody could discover the thief. Not a word was said by the woman about their growing possessions, for, in fact, the Vampire had menaced them with dreadful vengeance if they ever opened their lips on the subject. In other particulars the conduct of the Vampire was irreprehensible, and he was fond of talking with and caressing the girls. After about a month he had made himself quite at home in the house, where he passed all his nights, but departed at the dawn of day; when his widow, alarmed lest her conduct should be deemed sinful,

determined to consult the Papa (Greek priest) of the parish,
and to ask his counsel in so very embarrassing a state of
things. The Papa recommended her to be prudent, to avoid
any quarrel, but to endeavour to worm out from the Vampire
where he passed his time from sunrise to sunset—as it would
not be possible to destroy him in the churchyard, he having
been dead more than forty days. He even recommended her

to welcome him, to speak of him and act towards him with all kindness and affection, and to employ every winning art in order to ascertain where he went when he deserted her in the morning. The widow managed it all with so much dexterity that, after a few days, she was able to communicate to the Priest that her husband passed his days in the decayed trunk of a chestnut-tree—one of seven or eight which grew at a short distance from the village, on the north-east side. A communication was, therefore, made to the local authorities, and the usual permission was given. On the following Saturday the people collected, and surrounded the trees; but, as none of them were to appearance hollow, it was necessary to climb them—and on the top of one of the trunks, where it divided itself into branches, a large hole was discovered, and in that hole a dead body, standing erect, exhaling no disagreeable odour whatever. The ceremonies which have been described took place; the tree was cut down and burnt with the corpse.

"A proclamation was issued throughout the district that those who had lost anything should apply to the Turkish Commander, who would restore their property to them. He said that a great many people demanded things they had never lost, and that the most violent disputes took place between the various claimants. But he averred the exact truth of the facts, and added that the widow declared, before the competent tribunal, that the Vampire was cold as death, and that his touch was perfectly icy."

"Is it not very likely, Papa! that the widow was a receiver of stolen goods, and that, on detection, she invented the story of the Vampire?" said George.

"That may well be," answered Mr Howard; "for I believe, in nine cases out of ten, the belief in Ghosts, Genii, and Vampires is used in the East by clever rogues, as a means of carrying on and of concealing their fraudulent doings."

THE VAMPIRE OF VOURLA (1845)

Anonymous

"The Vampire of Vourla" appeared in the 1845 issue of The Chaplet:
An Elegant Literary Miscellany. *The date of publication appears
nowhere in the volume and is given in brackets in the online catalogs
of the libraries holding a copy. There is at least one other issue of this
obscure annual, also undated, so the publication as a whole remains
shrouded in a veil of mystery. The book brings together a number of
poems and stories with no author names except, occasionally, some
initials. That is not the case with this tale, published anonymously
in spite of its obvious quality, which aligns it with the best tradition
of mid-century ghost and horror stories. Its clever use of modern
narrative techniques, realistic setting, and conversational language
to convey a sense of sheer horror entitle it to claim an honored place
in the canon.*

*"Vourla" is the only, and the last, full-fledged Gothic narrative
featuring a Greek vampire after Polidori. Appearing in the same year
as the first installments of the bestseller* Varney the Vampire, *it
anticipates by more than fifty years several distinctive features from*
Dracula. *Actually, it does so to such an extent that it makes one
wonder whether Stoker was somehow aware of it. Worth noting are
the secluded mansion of the vampire, the mysterious servants who
transport her lover there every night in a boat and, above all, her
pioneering transformation into a huge bat that allows her to visit her
victim 'at home' to suck his blood. For all these reasons, but especially
for the latter, it might not be too farfetched to argue that the discovery
of this story compels us to reconsider, and perhaps in part to rewrite,
the whole history of 19th-century vampire fiction.*

Beyond this, note the semi-colonial context of the narrative, probably set among the geopolitical turbulences of the 1830s and '40s surrounding the Eastern Question. At that time, the British Navy was often sent to the Southeastern Mediterranean to conduct surveillance tasks as one of the Great Powers in charge of the international status quo. In 1839, in fact, Prime Minister Palmerston even dispatched a fleet to bombard the Syrian coast, recently occupied by the Egyptian Mehmet Ali at the expense of the Ottoman Empire. Lieutenant Somers, the protagonist of the narrative, was most likely a member of an expedition of that sort. However, the fact that Heira, the vampire, is largely described as an Ancient Greek who speaks "in the purest Ionic dialect" complicates the historical dimension of the story and makes it resonate with Polidori's warnings against the West's compulsive attraction to Greekness and the Hellenic ideal.

W ELL pleased with all the world, for nothing "passes along" good temper, from the captain down to the very powder-monkey, like a fair wind; we near the Sicilian coast, and if we have any luck shall reach Malta to-morrow. Now rises the towering Etna before us, apparently far inland, from off the southern coast of Sicily, but still perceptible. With what interest do we gaze on that mighty giant of the earth girt by eternal snows; its mouths of destruction yawning above fertile valleys, where the clinging vine entwines the olive, and the peasant toils unfearingly till the flood of flame comes, and the rain of ruin falls. Night closes over sea and shore. The wind has gone down considerably. The sails scarcely feel the light breeze, and idly flap on the masts. "The watch" is called: last night we took our "yarn" from before the mainmast; to-night we will join the "jollies" under the "half deck."

"Now, Lawyer Tom, give us the yarn about your master, Lieutenant Somers, and the black-boat, and that 'ere young 'oman what made him lose the number of his mess." This request was preferred to a marine, who, the watch having been mustered, was just thinking about taking "a cork;" but

he roused himself, and seeing around him a knot of his particular chums, he, after a little persuasion, consented. Let us
premise, before Tom Gahan begins, that he was not called
lawyer merely because he might be classed with that species
of the genus off "the rolls," serving afloat, men foremost at
written representations, and "round-robins," who, though
they have had a smattering of education, will not take no for a
negative, asking the meaning of orders meant only to be peremptory, and standing up on all occasions for what "Jack" calls
his "blasted rights:" no, Gahan had a further claim to the name
of lawyer, he had been a lawyer's clerk. Drink had proved
his ruin,—it had hastened his departure from several sets of
chambers—often had he rolled down the stairs; and on more
than one occasion, he had received a trifling assistance from
an angry employer's toe. At length, the seams of Tom's black
coat were of a most *unseemly* white, while the shirt that peeped
out from his elbows was marvellously yellow; and the lawyer's
clerk, not knowing where else to get a shilling, took one from
a recruiting sergeant, and listed for a royal marine—passed his
drills, and disliking the regular routine of his duties, became
an officer's servant. He had several times changed masters,—
through the circumstance of Chubb's locks being seldom
applied to spirit cases, which gentlemen often want to open in
a hurry,—at last there was a black mark made against his name
in the books of his company, and he was no longer allowed to
be a servant. Tom now took warning, and became moderately
sober; he even looked for advancement in the service, but alas!
he got the name of a "sea-lawyer:" this was a bar to his pro-
motion,—truth to say, borrowing a yankey expression, he was
"considerable litigious." A full private he remained, and in this
capacity we find him telling his yarn under the "half deck."

"I have declared more than once," said Tom the lawyer,
"that I'd rather not talk about poor Mr. Somers, but you go on
for ever boring one."

"Because we never heard the rights of the story," cried several voices—"yes, that's what it is."

"Well, then, here's to begin," rejoined Gahan, "but, remember I'll never tell it again, for I don't like the subject; talking about it makes a man sleep uneasy in his hammock when he turns in; but you will have it, and so here goes: I embarked with Lieutenant Somers, as his servant, when I had been just four years in the service, which I take it is nearly six years ago—worse luck to me! It's a service that there is nothing to be got by for a man who has had an education such as I have had, and who has associated with gentlemen."

"Never mind *that* part of the story," exclaimed one of Tom's audience, for "the lawyer" had a well known habit of expatiating on his fallen estate. This interruption had nearly spoilt the yarn altogether.

"If I've any of your sauce," he replied, turning to the offender, "I won't say another word;" but the general silence that ensued giving promise of more respectful attention, he thus continued. "Lieutenant Somers was a very gentlemanly-like officer; and at the time I am speaking of his embarking with *me* in his Majesty's ship ———, he might have been about two-and-twenty. We were ordered on this station, went to Malta, joined the fleet, and in less than ten days we were detached with other ships on a cruise to the eastward; and after awhile we all brought up in Vourla Bay. This you must know, those who don't know it already, is in the Gulf of Smyrna; and our anchorage was between fifteen and twenty miles from the city of that name; a beautifully wooded coast running up to it on each side of the Gulf, with here and there an island which would form a very pretty property in the British Channel; while in that country, I believe, no one cares to own them, but the partridges and the rabbits. Well, here we lay for nearly six weeks, and my master went every now and then up to Smyrna, for he was very fond of going about, and mixed a great deal with the people of the country: he had been several years on the station before, and spoke the Greek language, and I dare say made himself very agreeable to the ladies, for he was a fine handsome young fellow. To describe him, I should say that he was about my height, neither too tall nor too short, but just what a man ought to be. His hair was of a beautiful glossy brown it might be a shade lighter than mine;—it curled naturally, and so would my hair curl too, if that old captain of ours didn't keep us to such a soldier's crop; forgetting that there may be men amongst us who have been in the situation of gentlemen, and are, perhaps, as good as himself."

"Halloo Tom," from several voices, was answered by his repeating the threat—

"If you interrupt me I won't say a word more;—perhaps you don't care to hear the story—only tell me so—that's all. Well, to go on, if my master was not up at Smyrna, whenever he could get on shore he was shooting in the woods along the coast of the Gulf, and a capital shot he was—I could only just beat him. We had been about three weeks at Vourla, when every body remarked a sudden change in Mr. Somers' manner. He who used to be the life and soul of the wardroom-mess, was now silent and thoughtful: he lost his appetite, and would sit for hours together at table without doing more than answering the questions put to him, and parrying the jokes of his mess mates, who told him that he was either in love or in debt. He certainly was sometimes as moody as a man whose tailor would give him no more credit. I know what it is to feel after that fashion myself, when I've been obliged to give up going to a pleasant party, and disappoint all the girls who have been looking out for me, because I had not a proper coat to appear in. This is a kind of thing that may happen to any gentleman, but it could not have been the cause of the low spirits of my master, for he had plenty of money and was not in debt. What's more, if you watched him narrowly, you might see, now and then, a sort of quiet smile stealing over his face, as if he were thinking of something pleasant; but still that face of his was getting paler and paler every day. Mr. Somers had by this time quite given up joining the parties that went to Smyrna, nor did he ever go shooting, and seldom out of the ship in the day time; but regularly every night a boat fetched him about 'seven bells,' in the first watch, at least I know it was always near twelve o'clock. My master would ask to go on shore before he went down to his cabin in the cock-pit, and there he sat all by himself till the corporal of the guard came and told him that the boat was alongside. I've been on the look-out, for my hammock hung close to the entrance port, and I've seen Mr. Somers wrapped in his cloak going over the side, and I've turned out and ran up to the 'head' to get a sight of the boat. It seemed a kind of caïque, rowed by two rowers, and looked much like the common ones that we saw about, except that there was an awning spread in the stern-sheets, and that not a white one, but of a dark colour. I've heard the sentries and non-commissioned officers say it was quite black; but the boat has always been too far off by the time I got on deck, for me to speak certain on this point. In a few minutes she would be out of sight, and only the bright shining of the water, look-ing like flames as her prow cut the waves, showed how fast she was leaving the ship, nor was she ever seen again till just about gun-fire, at day-light. Then, almost before the sentries could hail her, there was the same caïque alongside, and Mr. Somers, looking as the corporals at the entrance port said, more like a corpse than a living man, he was so pale, would come on board: staggering with weakness, or, they hinted, it might be with drink, he would, at once, go down to his cabin. Now such a way of proceeding every night for nearly a fortnight set me thinking what it could all mean. I took it into my head that my master had an intrigue on his hands, and knowing how jealous both Greeks as well as Turks are of their wives and daughters, every morning when I went to call him I expected to find that he had not come back. Several of the men had disappeared on the station lately, but the common sailors and private marines are always supposed to have 'run' their ships, for your nobs never *can* suppose it possible that a marine or a foremast-man may get into a scrape and have his wizen cut; a circumstance rather preventing his coming back to his leave. Oh, no!—there's always an 'R' put against his name, and no more thought taken of it; but there's a shindy when an officer's missing: and a shindy I thought there would soon be about poor Mr. Somers. Well, as I was saying, all this went on night after night for nearly a fortnight, and mighty curious was I to find out the rights of it. Once or twice I just said to my master in the morning, 'you had a rough or a fine night for your row, sir, last night,' as the case might have been, just to sound him, but he would bite his lip and frown, never answering me; and then he would tell me to give him something that he wanted angrily, and I didn't like to try it on. However, as it happened, one night I got my wish, in a manner that I didn't expect. I had been busy helping a mess-mate, the gun-room steward, putting things to rights in the midshipmen's berth, which—the young gentlemen messing altogether in the gun-room,—was used as a sort of a store-room or pantry, and there had been a flare-up party that day given by the middies. This berth was next to my master's cabin; and just as I was coming out, I heard him, and a great chum of his, a Lieutenant of the navy, called Hardy, go in. The steward had left me alone, for there was enough to do in the gun-room, where the officers had not yet finished their jollification, so I had only to douse the light, keep quiet, and put my ear to the door of the 'wing,' between the berth and the cabin, to hear what the gentlemen said, just the same as though I had been alongside of them. That night I listened to a story which I shall never forget; and, from what happened afterwards, I suppose I know more about poor Mr. Somers than any man living. I'll tell you just word for word what passed, which I can do, having written it out while the thing was fresh in my memory; this is no place to read in, but I believe I have the whole thing pretty well by heart. 'And so you think I am looking ill, Hardy,' said my master. 'Ill!' answered the naval Lieutenant, 'I never saw a fellow looking worse; and 'tis not I only who remark it, but every one in the ward-room. If you don't take care you'll be going off the hooks, and leaving your bones at Vourla.' 'It may be so,' returned Mr. Somers, yet speaking cheerfully, 'and I would as soon make my grave on these wooded shores, as in some formal, though quite as ill-guarded burial ground in England; but I'm not going to die just at present—life has too many charms for me.' 'You must take care of your health, then, or life's charms will not keep life in you,' said Mr. Hardy. 'Here you go away night after night on your mysterious excursions, all weathers—the very dew often falling like rain, and every day you are looking worse and worse. Somers! these midnight trips must be given up,— there is no use in mincing the matter. You know the friendship I have for you. We were old messmates before we met on board here, and I can't bear to see you killing yourself, without speaking. The doctor said honestly the other day when I asked him about you, that to look at your case superficially,—for you have never given him an opportunity of judging a bit more than the rest of us—he should be inclined to believe that you are falling into a state of confirmed atrophy; and so my good fellow, if you don't look out you'll lose the number of your mess, and make us lose a pleasant messmate.'"

"What ship is that Superficale," and "what's confarming a man to the Trophy, when there ain't such a ship in the sarvice," asked two of Tom the lawyer's listeners.

"Hold your jaw," said Tom, "and let me tell the story as it should be told, or I won't tell it at all. My master, I fancied, was lost in thought for a moment, and then as it seemed with a sudden start, he exclaimed, 'Hardy, you shall be informed of all, and judge for me. I know that I am ill—I feel feverish and bewildered. I sometimes think that I am living in the midst of a strange dream, and that I must one day awake and find that all the past is a fantasy—but you shall hear: I can trust you—I know you will not mention what I am about to reveal, out of this cabin.' Mr. Hardy said all that was proper in reply, and then my master began. 'You are aware that my love of shooting has often taken me miles and miles away from the ship, and that many a night it has been very late before I have come on board. It was on one of these excursions that I found myself high up on the southern coast of the Gulf, and, as I imagined, more than ten miles from our anchorage. The sun was setting, and the caïque that I had hired was to meet me at what we call the agate-wall watering-place. As I walked along, the sudden gathering of darkness around, made it plain to me that a storm was brewing, and I had hardly gone more than half a mile farther, when the falling of a few heavy drops of rain showed me that it was time to look for shelter, while the thunder, and the echoes of the thunder kept up one contin-ued roar, as if the whole fleet was at general exercise. I was on the point of getting under a tree, to remain there at all risks till the storm was past, when I saw a light in the distance; it appeared to be inland, but whether caused by a fire in the woods, or proceeding from some house,—and few indeed, as you know, are the habitations there about,—it was impossi-ble to tell. But any port in a storm;—there was a chance of getting under a roof, and I pushed my way through the trees until I came right upon an ancient looking building, a wing of which I had almost ran against, as I leaped through a thicket of myrtles and brambles, before I was aware of it. I now saw that from a projecting window, partially latticed, and situated high up in an opposite corner of the house, the light proceeded. The heavy rain drops were thickening fast; I expected every moment that a torrent would fall from the heavens. It was no time to stand upon ceremony, so I at once made up to a large door that was before me, and finding neither knocker nor bell meet my hand, as I felt eagerly for some means of arousing the inhabitants to claim their hospitality; I was about to make the butt of my gun answer the purpose, when the door swung back. By the twilight of sunset, which still struggled against the darkness of the storm, I could just perceive that it gave me admittance to a sort of square court-yard; overhanging this were latticed windows of a similar description to the one out-side the building, whence came the light I before mentioned. After looking about to discover who it was that let me in, but without effect, it occurred to me that by some contrivance, communicating with the upper part of the house, the latch might have been lifted, or perhaps I had only to thank the violence of the wind for my entrance. I was cogitating about this, and making up my mind whether I should prosecute the adventure I had begun by seeking some way of getting into the interior of the habitation, or content myself with the shelter I had already obtained under one of the latticed projections, when the sound of a stringed instrument played by a very skilful finger, completely upset the pros and cons of my deliberation. Never had I before heard so touching a strain, as was the short symphony which preluded a still more enthralling witchery of melody: a voice, that seemed by its sweetness to hush the very storm, sung a plaintive Greek song. Both the air and words were new to me—together, for the music spoke the sentiment of the poetry—they told of death in youth, when, the warm life-blood suddenly chilled by the destroyer, those who love the departed lament how short has been their sojourn on earth: scarcely believing they are "not," we see them return in dreams. The husband again feels the cheek of his wife pillowed on his bosom—the lover again presses to his heart her, who, blighting the promise of his expected joys, had made her bridal-bed in the cold grave. And then there came a change in the song: it told of pale ghosts that beckon the living to join the dead, and of midnight whisperings, in which familiar voices breathe the accents of the loved and lost. Ere the strain had ceased—scarcely knowing how I had made my way into the house, so perfectly bewildered did I feel,—I was hastening up a marble staircase guided by the sound of the melody, while a soft light, proceeding from a chamber on the landing-place immediately above me, showed me the path I was pursuing. The next moment I had rushed past the portals from whence the music came, and then all was still as death. I had entered a sort of ante-chamber to a larger apartment,— no one was there, and on I went. I felt not the least embarrassment at thus intruding on the privacy of strangers;—I really believe that music had maddened me:—another door was passed. The room I now arrived at was laid with Persian carpeting of the richest colours; silken hangings concealed the walls, and on pedestals of bronze, silver lamps were burning the most fragrant oils, dispensing at once light and perfume all around. There was a kind of divan, or sofa, at the end of the apartment, and on one of its cushions I saw the lyre,—but the minstrel had fled. I told you before, Hardy, that I believe I was not in my right senses, and this must account for what I now did: I snatched up the instrument;—I apostrophized it aloud; I besought it to bring back its mistress; I wildly swept its chords, then dashed it on the divan and gazed around me with the air of a man who looks for something whereon to vent his spleen in the excess of disappointment. The movement of a silken curtain attracted my attention—a little hand appeared—the drapery was withdrawn, and a being of such exquisite beauty came forth, that for a moment I stood entranced.'"

"Snore! snore! nore! snore! nore!"

"The brute!" exclaimed Tom the lawyer, interrupted in his story, and looking bayonets at a sleeping comrade, whose nose expressed as plainly as nose could, that its proprietor was asleep. Pacified by the declaration of his remaining auditors that they were all attention, private Gahan, who had now got into the spirit of his yarn, and told it more for his own pleasure than to please others, proceeded.

"Well, my master said that never had he beheld such a lovely creature before. She appeared to be a Greek in all the ripe charms of womanhood. Her hair flowed down her shoulders in long graceful curls, crowned by a little scarlet cap, embroidered with gold, and further ornamented by a tassel of purple silk. Lustrous were her deep hazel eyes, and Mr. Somers declared that he felt as though they looked into his very soul. The beautiful stranger wore a vest of the darkest marone colour, under which was a silken petticoat of scarlet and white stripe, gathered in very full at the waist, and descending in heavy folds of drapery until it met the finely turned ankles, clothed only in their own dazzling whiteness: and then her little feet and little yellow slippers!—Oh! my master seemed as if he would never have done talking about them, for he had always a great fancy for a pretty foot. When this lovely young Greek had advanced into the middle of the room,—which she did treading lightly, smiling and holding up her finger warningly, as if to entreat silence,—she addressed Mr. Somers in the most bewitchingly soft tones; but I had better give you his own words, as nearly as I can. Those who want to go to sleep may; only let the last one whistle when he's off for the land of nod. I can't tell a story like an old quarter-master yarning—it is not fit that I should, or what's the use of having had a good education, and having lived among gentlemen, before I entered to serve with you fellows."

"Why didn't you stay where you was," grumbled out a distant voice—Mr. Gahan, *of course!* never heard this rude speech, and thus went on.

" 'Hardy,' said my master, 'not a word did she speak till she got into the centre of the apartment, and then the sweetest tones that ever met my ear, in the purest Ionic dialect almost whispered, "Why are you here? You are in danger—you know not the danger that threatens you. Why do you tempt your fate?" "I care not what my fate may be," said I, "content I shall be with it, so that I am but allowed to gaze upon thy beauty." She did not seem angry when I thus spoke, but cast her eyes on the ground, while I explained to her, how, driven by the storm to seek shelter in the court-yard of the house, I had been led onward, taking the music of her voice for my guide, until it had brought me into her presence. As I ceased speaking, she looked up with such a radiant smile that I lost all command over myself, and rushing forward I seized her hand and poured forth the most ardent expressions of admiration. I swore eternal fidelity to her;—besought her to sanction my loving her,—and, I dare say, uttered a great deal of nonsense. Be that as it might, all I advanced was well received, for unresistingly she allowed me to lead her to the divan, and seat myself beside her. "Then you love me—you swear to love no other,—to be all mine?" said Heira, for thus she told me to call her, when we had long sat hand in hand, looking into each other's eyes, as if we there read the secrets of the soul. My arm crept round her waist; she shrunk not from me. I felt her tremble, as though shaken by the quick pulse of her heart beating beneath the thin muslin kerchief that hid her bosom, and my head bowed on her shoulder: she cast her arms around me,—the faltering words, "can I trust you?" were whispered in my ear; "Will you swear by your life-blood? Will you mingle it with mine? Will you pledge with me to our eternal fidelity?" She had without my perceiving it drawn a dagger from her girdle, for my eyes were still fixed on hers, as I looked up from my sweet resting place. I felt the sleeve of my coat torn open, my arm bared. "What would you that we should do?" I exclaimed, for a moment starting from her embrace. "It is an ancient custom of our race," she replied; "Let us mingle our blood; then shall we be as one life, living but for each other—sharing the same bliss—dying the same death." Oh! Hardy, the soft radiance of those eyes when she thus spake. I held out my arm—had it been on the instant to break up the fountains of life, I should have consented. I felt the blood trickle from my vein;—it fell into a crystal bowl. I can tell no more: I know not what followed with any degree of certainty. I have a sort of confused recollection that when her arm was pierced no blood flowed, and that I shudderingly saw the ruby of her lips become of a deeper tint, as she pledged to our union "for ever and for ever!"—but I believe it was all a dream: I had sunk on her bosom—I forgot all but that she was mine.'

" ' "We are to meet again," said the lovely stranger, as the first streak of dawn appeared in the sky that had hung as a dark curtain before the open lattice of our chamber. "Oh! that we might never part!" I answered, "but tell me how are we to meet?" "At night I will send for you," rejoined Heira; "be ready—a boat will come to your ship." "You know it, then," I rejoined. "Did I not know you—did I not know your abiding-place, you would not now be here," she remarked. All this passed at our parting, and, strange as it may appear to you, I did not further question her. Heira hurried my departure;—she looked fearfully at the coming dawn, as though she dreaded the approach of some intruder. Tearing myself from her embrace, I once more descended the stairs of the mysterious mansion. I met no one—I crossed the court-yard, opened the door, and going forth perceived to my surprise, through the branches of the trees, the waters of the Gulf at a little distance from me: the night before, it had appeared as though I had left them far behind. The sun was scarcely yet above the waves, but there was the promise of a lovely day; the storm had long passed. I walked on toward the sea, and, as though I were still in a strange dream, I had been some time in the Smyrna road ere I perceived where I was; nor could I from that hour to this discover at what point I came into it. I felt feverish and languid—I looked at my arm and a faintness crept over me. There was the punctured vein, but the blood had ceased to flow. I roused myself, and tried to call to mind the events of the last night:—I could not collect my thoughts—visions of horror and bliss seemed confusedly blended, for if I shuddered as I pictured to myself Heira's lips pressed to that blood-red bowl, this was forgotten in the remembrance of that moment when those lips were first pressed to mine. The sun was rising high in the heavens, when the boatmen of a caïque returning from Smyrna hailed me. They doubtlessly imagined that I had need of their assistance; I must have looked way-worn and weary. The sleeve of my coat was ripped to the shoulder, and I held my fowling-piece with but a feeble grasp. You remember the state of exhaustion I was in when I came on board, and your surprise, indeed the surprise of everyone, when I expressed my determination of going on shore again. That same night a boat came for me as was promised by Heira. I spoke to the rowers, who appeared to be Greeks, but they either could not or would not understand me—they returned me no answer. Their caïque is an extremely fleet one, for it always seems to me that I am a very short space of time beneath its sombre awning, ere we run in-shore, and up a creek which brings me within a hundred yards of my destination. Well, Hardy, this has gone on for ten days. I have no fear that any harm is intended me in the strange habitation to which I resort. Heira does not now even affect any alarm on my account, except that about an hour before day light she tells me that I must depart: I find the same boat and boatmen awaiting me, and silently and swiftly I am conveyed on board. Now you have all my extraordinary story: people say I am ill, and that I am tri-fling with my constitution, but they are thoroughly mistaken. I may suffer a little from broken rest, but that is all. No! there is one thing I must mention,—sometimes I fancy that the vein of my arm has bled afresh amid the deep slumber from which Heira awakes me, to tell me I must leave her. It never heals, and the puncture has always an appearance of freshness.' My master here showed his arm to Mr. Hardy," continued Gahan, "but I could not exactly make out what the naval Lieutenant now said; he seemed to hum and haw over it. When I could next understand what was going on, he was cautioning Mr. Somers; telling him that he had better take care that his amour did not end in robbery, perhaps murder; and asking him whether he had ever tried by daylight to discover the house in which his mysterious meetings with the Greek girl took place. My master answered the warning of his friend by saying, that he felt assured no kind of danger was to be apprehended. Heira seemed to have full command of the habitation: an ele-gant repast always awaited his arrival, though no attendants were to be seen; and, as he had already said, till the hour before daylight, when he was bidden to depart, the lovely Greek showed not the slightest appearance of alarm, and on her faith he could not but implicitly rely. With respect to seeking out their place of assignation in the day time, Mr. Somers declared that he had tried every means in his power. He had loitered near the house, instead of at once descending to the caïque; but Heira's hand waved impatiently from the latticed window, ever commanding his departure, while his boatmen would approach and silently point to the shore: he had even coasted the whole of the southern side of the Gulf, hoping to discover the creek he nightly ascended, but without effect."

"'And you really will proceed with this affair!' asked Mr. Hardy.

"'To the death,' replied my master, 'as surely as seven bells strike to-night, so surely will my boat come, and I go. Knowing that Heira expects me, can I fail in my pledge to her?'

"There was now a pause in the conversation between the gentlemen.

"'I cannot make it out,' at length said Mr. Hardy, as if he had been in a brown study.

"'There is nothing to make out, except that I am a very lucky fellow,' rejoined my master, laughing. 'There, go away, and don't puzzle your head about it—I want to get an hour's sleep, if I can: I need not remind you of your promise to keep secret what you have just heard;—to no other but yourself, would I have breathed it.' Again Mr. Hardy cautioned his friend to be careful of himself—not only of his life, lest any harm should be intended him—but of his health, evidently suffering from broken rest, and the feverish excitement in which he lived, and after a while, the naval Lieutenant went away. I then let myself out of the berth where I had so snugly lain; and only just in time, for the steward was coming down to know why I did not bring him the key of it; and the young gentlemen, having broken up in the gun-room, were beginning to turn into their hammocks. That night my master went away in the boat as usual, and the next morning I found him lying in his bed-place looking pale as death itself. He now, for the first time, complained that he was ill. 'Gahan,' said he, 'I am not well. You must get me a cup of tea from the ward-room. I feel too weak to go to breakfast: I believe, I have taken cold. Don't say a word to any one about it, only ask Mr. Johnson to take my guard for me.' This was a brother subaltern of his, who being good-natured, took most of my master's duties, for he was, what is called, a 'regular ship-keeper.' Well, I just did what Mr. Somers told me. I had intended to do more, but scarcely had I given my master his breakfast when an accident occurred that prevented me. I meant to tell Mr. Hardy how ill his friend was, and ask him whether he hadn't better at once send the doctor to him. The signal had been made for the fleet to exercise sails,—poor Mr. Hardy was on the forecastle, and a block came from aloft, struck him right on the top of his head, and fractured his skull:—he never spoke again, and died in less than three days after. Whether it was hearing what had happened to Mr. Hardy made my master worse, or not, I can't tell; but before the people's dinner-time, he was in a high fever. The doctor came, and then it was, as they tried to bleed him, that I saw, what I had heard him mention,—the vein in his arm unhealed, as if it had been just opened. I say the doctor tried to bleed him, for the blood would hardly flow at all, and astonished our surgeon was, though not so particularly at this, as at finding that Mr. Somers had been so lately bled—asking him about it was no manner of use, for he was talking quite at random, and I couldn't exactly tell what I knew, without telling how I heard it, which would have been awkward. A screen-berth was now rigged up for my master on the middle deck. He was put into a hot bath; once more they tried to bleed him, and at length, they got a little blood. He was then laid in his cot, and it was my office to sponge him over with vinegar and water. Still the fever got a-head, and the doctor didn't seem to like the case. I offered to take the first turn at sitting up with my master. He was now quite delirious, and talked wildly of a beautiful Syren bringing him to his death. Then he would extend his arms, and smiling languidly, almost in a whisper say that it was bliss thus to die: and once, suddenly bursting into a cry of agony, he exclaimed, 'There! there! Destroy me not! Monster! take, oh take those lips away! they are red with my blood. Is this, then, your love for me?' I spoke to him, and put my hand on his, telling him that there was no one near him except myself: he took no kind of notice of me, but from exhaustion, he ceased his cries. I gave him a composing draught, which he drank eagerly, about five bells in the middle watch; after this, he did not say much, and at last he sank into a sort of doze. I suppose it was the sight of my master drinking that made me thirsty. I felt uncommonly dry, and as I had brought up most of Mr. Somers' things from the cock-pit, of course I hadn't forgotten the liquor-case. There it was, and the bunch of keys on the table—a regular help-yourself-chance. I couldn't find any rum;—I always like it best, when I have the mixing of it;—but I got hold of some brandy, and I took a stiff glass of grog. Perhaps it was the smell of the vinegar, and the work I had gone through all day long that was too much for me, but while I was thinking over the strange things my master had been talking about, I dropped into a sound nap, quite forgetting that I ought to have been keeping a good look-out.

"I dare say, it must have been close upon the end of the first watch,—as near midnight as well could be—that I was awoke by a sort of flapping and flapping, just as if some one was fanning with a large fan, as they do in the East Indies. I could hardly open my eyes at first, I was so drowsy. There was a port in the screen-berth, and the sash was thrown back on the gun, for the weather was very hot, and a draught of wind had flared the sperm candle on the table down to a mere snuff; thus when I *did* look about me, I could not for a moment discover all that was going on, but never shall I forget what I at last made out. My master was lying motionless in the cot, his eyes wide open—staring at the hideous form of a large bat, nearly as large as some I have seen in the island of Java—there they call them *Vampires*—and oh! what a head it had! I could almost fancy that I saw human, or rather a devil's features, in those small bright eyes, and quickly working jaws, as these last, close-pressed to my master's neck, were drawing, drawing, drawing, the life-blood from his sinking frame, while the dark leathern wings fanned as the creature sucked. I suppose I must have called out. I certainly aimed a blow at the monster, for I caught my hand against the case-bottle of brandy and down it went. Altogether there was such a row, that the sentry outside came in: the doctor was sent for by the officer of the watch, while I was declared to be drunk and put in irons. I could swear that I never felt more sober in all my life; but had our skipper happened to be one of your flogging-men, I should certainly have got three dozen in the morning; as it was, they stopped my grog for a month. Before I was let out of irons,—aye, before the next night, poor Mr. Somers died. I begged hard to see him, but I wasn't allowed. I didn't say anything about the bat, for fear of getting into a worse scrape than I was in: but I asked the carpenter's-mate, who was a chum of mine, afterwards, if he didn't see something like a bite in my master's neck, when he and the carpenter measured the corpse for its coffin. The man declared that he had taken particular notice of a sort of red mark nearly under the right ear, and that he had heard the doctor saying to the First Lieutenant, that it was apiece with the rest of the affair, and very strange altogether. They had buried my poor master before I got my liberty, so I never could make out any more about it, and I generally keep what I know to myself, only to-night as you asked me:"—Tom the lawyer turned to look at his companions, for he had been latterly leaning against a stanchion of the deck, heedless who was listening.

"What had that ere young homan to do with that ere big Bat, what you calls a *Wampire?* and what became of that ere young homan after all?" inquired the little drummer, who had crept into the group unnoticed, and was a *solitary* listener.

All Mr. Gahan's chums, overpowered by the beauty of his narrative, had gone fast asleep. "Come out of that, you young sheepskin fiddler," exclaimed the enraged story-teller, "and be off to your hammock, or I'll make you!"

THE VROUCOLACAS: A TALE (1839)

James K. Paulding

The only American piece of this collection appeared in the 1846 issue of Graham's Magazine *(1840-1858), an entertainment journal based in Philadelphia containing fiction, music, photographs, book reviews, and general information. Its readership were men and women from both popular and more refined audiences. Among its editors was Edgar Allan Poe (1841-42), some of whose best-known short stories, such as "The Murders in the Rue Morgue," were first published in this magazine. James K. Paulding (1778-1860), the author of the narrative we present here, was an American writer and politician who even served as the United States Secretary of the Navy between 1838 and 1841. As a writer, Paulding, Washington Irving's friend and collaborator, was primarily considered a humorist, which is significant of the gradual relegation of the Greek vampires to 'minor', non-Gothic or non-horror genres. Indeed, "The Vroucolacas: A Tale" seems to parody Polidori's 1819 novel from its very title. It is basically a scathing Orientalist satire that mocks Eastern society and traditions from a pedestal of colonial superiority. In that sense, the narrative does not spare the Greeks, depicted once more as an integral part of the debauched Orient. Although Paulding proves to be admirably familiar with the milestones of 18th-century non-fictional* vrykolakas *literature—the description of the vampire craze in the city is an almost literal reproduction of the French writer Joseph Pitton de Tournefort's renowned account of the 1701 epidemic in Mykonos—he turns vampirism into just a mark of the Greeks' superstition and dishonesty. From that point of view, the story follows the steps of "The Vampire Knight" and of Bowring's chapter, only in an even more pungent tone.*

E VERY classical reader is doubtless familiar with the celebrated Island of Crete, where flourished the illustrious Minos, the pattern of judges; where Jupiter was cradled on Mount Ida; where the great labyrinth exhibited its inextricable windings; where the wine was super-excellent, and the people, according to all ancient authorities, no better than they should be. In the various mutations of this world, the island has changed its name to that of Candia, and the government of Minos for that of the representative of the Prophet. But the wine and the people remain as they were, one fit for the gods, the other for the penitentiary. They fear nothing but the Turks, the Corsairs, and the Vroucolacas.

When a Christian dies in Candia, they cannot afford him Christian burial without giving ten pence to the paps, or priest, two crowns to the bishop, and double that sum to the grand-vicar, the arch-treasurer, and the archivist; nay, it goes hard but the Patriarch of Constantinople comes in for a share. If these things are neglected, ten to one but the unfortunate deceased becomes a Vroucolacas, which, in the modern Greek jargon, signifies the spectre of a dead body possessed by a demon. They are always mischievous, and not unfrequently malignant, according to the previous character of the person they represent, playing all sorts of tricks, and occasionally indulging in cruel, unseemly amusements, not unlike the witches and necromancers of old, as certified by undoubted authority, ecclesiastical, civil and judicial. Having recorded these indispensable preliminaries, we shall now proceed with our tale.

More than a century ago there resided in the city of Candia, capital of the island of that name, and famous in history for sustaining one of the most obstinate sieges on record, a very dignified person of Latin extraction, who either was, or pretended to be, descended not only from the ancient Dukes of the Archipelago, but the Greek Emperors of Constantinople, and carried his head erect accordingly, except in the presence of a turban. Among his down-trodden and oppressed race he gave himself great airs of superiority, but the sight of a turban instantly converted him into a cringing slave, and a visit from a janizary gave him a fit of the ague. His name was Crispo Sanudo; he possessed a house in the city, highly creditable to a people that knew nothing of architecture, and a garden containing abundance of citron, lemon, orange, olive and pomegranate trees, planted without the least regard to order or regularity, and looking very much like a little wilderness. Besides, he paid the highest tax of any inhabitant of the whole island, except the Superior of the Monastery of Arcadi, the monks of which, as is the case all the world over, and more especially in the Grecian Archipelago, possessed the richest lands, and the finest olive and labdanum trees in Candia. In addition to all this, he, as before stated, boasted of having in his veins a sprinkling of the blood of the Comnenii Emperors of Constantinople, the meanest race that ever occupied the throne of the Cæsars. Every thing else that was Greek he despised, but still he gloried in being descended from Michael the Stammerer, whose daughter had married one of his ancestors, a Duke of the Archipelago, of the family of Sanudo.

But his most valuable possession was an only child, a daughter called Florentia, now just on the eve of finished womanhood, and the fairest of all the daughters of the isle. It was a great reflection, however, on her intellect, that she was quite blind to the foibles of her father, and her own beauties, both which were universally acknowledged. But the truth is, she was kept so close that she had no opportunity of comparing him with any body but her old nurse, and a young man she had more than once seen through the lattice of her window, gazing at her with looks peculiarly expressive. Crispo was proud of his daughter, for he had loved her deceased mother as well as a selfish man can love any thing but himself; and, besides this, she was docile as a lamb, and descended from the Greek emperors—not forgetting Michael the Stammerer.

Florentia, though confined to her cage, was as lively as a Canary bird, and tripped about the castle, as Signor Crispo called it, till she was tired, after which she sung the old nurse to sleep with the voice of a seraph, though the poor soul had almost entirely lost her hearing, in her youth, by the tremendous cannonading of the Knights Templars at the siege of Candia. The young Grecian maid was indeed very happy until she attained the age of sixteen, for such innocent beings can be happy almost anywhere. About this time, however, an event occurred, which, in its consequences, led to a gradual interruption of that serenity and repose she had hitherto enjoyed.

She was frequently permitted to walk in the garden, which was surrounded by a pretty high wall, accompanied sometimes by her father, but generally by her old nurse, who was wonderfully addicted to dozing in warm weather, and who, in that state, could only be roused by an exemplary shaking. On one of these occasions, as Florentia was standing under an orange tree laden with the choicest fruit, there suddenly fell at her feet one of the most beautiful pomegranates she had ever seen. She picked it up, and admired, and inhaled its delicious odors, when all at once it occurred to her to wonder whence it came. The tree under which she stood did not certainly bear such fruit, and yet the pomegranate as certainly fell from the tree. While in this state of perplexity, her wonder was changed to astonishment and dismay by a still more remarkable phenomenon. A man came tumbling down from the tree instead of a pomegranate, and having luckily escaped with his limbs whole, threw himself at the feet of Florentia, and looked in her face with such an air of profound humility that she could not but find in her heart to forgive his intrusion. Indeed she was so frightened at his first appearance that she uttered a faint scream, but it reached not the dozing nurse, who was reclining on a grassy terrace; and having at length ventured to look in the face of the new comer, she at once recognized the young man who had of late so frequently passed the house, gazing intently on the lattice of her window. She sometimes thought, and had dreamed of him two or three times, but her imagination had never gone further either sleeping or waking. She was at first highly offended at this most unceremonious visit; the next feeling was curiosity to know its motive, and this was soon gratified.

The jealous policy of the Orientals, which denies to women that salutary freedom to which all rational beings are fairly entitled, renders such meetings as this generally very brief and conclusive. The citadel must be carried by storm, or surprise, or it will be relieved to a certainty; and where young persons of different sexes are secluded from each other, the attraction of propinquity is almost irresistible. The young intruder was very handsome, and possessed all the fluent eloquence of a Greek. He declared his love, in an Oriental rhapsody, and besought her pity and forgiveness—in other words to return his affection. He announced himself as the son of Signor Constantachi, the oldest physician of the island, who was bred at the University of Padua, and had narrowly escaped the bastinado for having administered a dose of calomel to the Bashaw of Retisno, which made his mouth so sore that he could not smoke his pipe in peace. Being, however, deputy vice-consul for his Most Christian Majesty, the doctor pleaded his privilege, and was let off for a present of coffee and tobacco. The name of the young man was Miquelachi, or Michael, the *achi* being equivalent to a title of nobility. It is like the *De* of Europe, and indicates a descent from somebody.

Florentia, knowing that the old nurse would not sleep forever, and that no time was to be lost, modestly responded a gentle assent to the ardent solicitations of the enamored youth, just as the old woman was awakened by the sting of a bee, which had probably mistaken her face for a flower-bed, and, being disappointed, revenged himself in that manner. Miquelachi thereupon made a precipitate retreat among the trees of the garden, which, as before stated, formed a perfect wilderness, but not so quick as to escape the notice of the old nurse, whose sight was, however, none of the brightest, and who, rubbing her eyes as she came forward, declared she had seen either a man or a ghost flit before her, insisting at the same time on knowing who or what it was. It has long since been observed that the most innocent and sincere maiden, who never before dreamed of deceit or falsehood, will, when placed in the predicament of Florentia, be sorely tempted to the commission of both these grievous offences. Be this as it may, the young lady, though she did not absolutely deny the fact, insisted that the old nurse had become half blind, as well as half deaf, and dexterously, as she thought, turned her attention to the wonderful circumstance of a pomegranate falling from an orange tree.

As this is not a tale of love, we shall forbear to dwell minutely on the various steps in the progress of the intimacy between Miquelachi and Florentia, which, like all others on record, ended in a discovery. Though no more pomegranates dropped from the orange-tree, Miquelachi often made his appearance in the garden, while the old nurse was napping and Signor Crispo attending his vocations abroad, he being one of those men who are always busy about nothing. In a surprisingly short time a strong mutual affection grew up between the young people, who frequently discussed the expediency of either asking the signor's consent, or marrying without it. The first was rather a forlorn hope, the latter impossible, without absconding to some one of the neighboring islands. The old nurse, however, saved them the trouble of deciding, by one day awaking in a most miraculous manner half an hour before her time, and not only discovering the apparition was a man, but detecting his identity. No explanation was necessary; she comprehended the whole affair, and discreetly shutting her eyes, began to define her position; that is, to think seriously on the relative advantages of keeping the secret of Florentia, or discovering it to her father. She really had a strong regard for that young lady, but still more highly appreciated the comforts of her present situation. Finally, she came to the conclusion that the whole affair must come out some time or other, and the discovery ruin all her prospects in life, unless made by herself.

Accordingly she disclosed the whole matter to Signor Sanudo, whereby she roused all the blood of the Pascologii, the Comnenii—not forgetting Michael the Stammerer—and of the ancient Dukes of the Archipelago, into a fury. The illustrious descendant of these worthies despised, from the bottom of his soul, the Constantachi, Ianachi, Miquelachi, and all the other achis—whom he considered a pack of ignoble upstarts, though in truth they could claim a far nobler lineage than his own, being descended from the ancient proprietors of the island under the reign of King Minos, if all they said were true. Beside this general contempt, he had a special personal antipathy to Signor Constantachi. Being as ignorant as a caloyer or a papas, he cherished a peculiar hostility to every species of learning, and hated the worthy doctor because he had been educated at the University of Padua, and pretended to understand that detestable jargon, the ancient Greek language. Moreover, the family of Constantachi all belonged to the Greek church, and were tainted with the heresies of Eutychius, whose doctrines were condemned by the Council of Chalcedon, while Signor Crispo himself adhered to the Latin communion. Those who have so often seen, in the records of the past, that religion, which is all charity and love, made a pretext for the indulgence of all the malignant passions of the human mind, will not be surprised at being told that this difference, of the grounds and principles of which the signor was profoundly ignorant, except that one acknowledged the Pope of Rome, the other the Patriarch of Constantinople, should add greatly to the bitterness of his spleen and hatred. Finally, he was negotiating a marriage between Florentia and the son of a descendant of the noble family of Cornari in Venice.

All these excitements operating on a man who carried

more sail than ballast, raised his wrath to the highest pitch of ludicrous extravagance. He poured a deluge of reproaches on his daughter; threatened to tie the faithful old nurse in a sack and throw her into the sea, for not foreseeing this before it happened; invoked the shades of his ancestors—not forgetting Michael the Stammerer—to rise up and avenge the insult offered to their descendant; and after shutting up Florentia in a part of the house whence she could see nothing but the sky, proceeded majestically into his garden, where he ordered the tree which produced the forbidden fruit to be grubbed up by the roots. Not content with this, after serious reflection he resolved to lay his grievances before the Bashaw of Candia, and demand justice on the presumptuous intruder not only into his garden, but the heart of his daughter. Putting a purse of sequins in his pocket, he accordingly proceeded to execute his purpose.

The Bashaw was a hale, hearty old man, somewhat rising threescore, named Redschid, but commonly called Djezzar, or the butcher, in compliment to his taste for cutting off heads, and the inimitable skill as well as grace with which he performed that operation. He paid as little respect to the life of a human being, especially if not one of the Faithful, as to that of a swine, which all know every true disciple of the Prophet holds in utter abomination. There was nothing on earth Signor Crispo stood in such awe of as a Bashaw of Three Tails, especially one who, like Djezzar, could take off heads in the twinkling of an eye with a blow of his scimitar. His rage, however, on this occasion overcame his apprehensions, and he strutted boldly to the residence of the Bashaw, which was an old dilapidated castle built by the Venetians when masters of the island, and which had fallen into decay; it being against the conscience of a Turk to repair any thing. The Bashaws are appointed only for a brief period, and the chances are they will lose their heads before that expires. They, therefore, never do any thing for those who come after them. Djezzar was one day asked by a traveler why he did not repair his castle, which, in truth, kept out neither wind nor weather—"Mashallah!" replied he, "for what? I shall probably encounter a Hatta-Sheriff before long, and lose my head by the scimitar, or my breath by the bow-string. I should only be taking trouble for my successor. Allah Kerib—God is great, Mahomet is his Prophet, the Commander of the Faithful his representative, and I am his slave."

Crispo found this philosophical Bashaw sitting cross-legged, in a room, the roof of which let in daylight at various points, on a sofa, which, though almost the only furniture to be seen, was much the worse for wear. He was smoking a long pipe, the tube of which passed through a jar of cold water, in order to render the smoke more refreshing. On one side stood a slave fanning him; on the other lay his sabre of blue Damascus steel, which made Signor Crispo turn of the same color, in order that he might have it handy to cut off the head of the fanner if he suffered a fly to come within striking distance of his beard. The signor trembled to the very marrow of his bones at this formidable exhibition; but having bowed three times almost to the ground, the floor being literally nothing else, he summoned courage to relate his wrongs, but unluckily in his trepidation forgot the offering of the purse. The Bashaw heard him with becoming gravity, and then simply asked—

"Is thy daughter so beautiful as I have heard?"

Crispo felt his blood run cold at this question, for he well knew its purport. He answered, however, as promptly and firmly as possible—

"No, most illustrious Djezzar, she is the least beautiful of all the daughters of the city. But consider her noble descent—"

"Bah!" exclaimed Djezzar, interrupting him, contrary to the Oriental custom always to listen patiently till a story is finished—"Bah! what is all that? I am myself the son of a Georgian slave, yet I command half this island, and you among the rest, though you pretend to a descent from those recreant Christian emperors whom the representatives of the Prophet scattered before them like so many Christian dogs, as they were. Why talk of thy forefathers? Thou didst not beget them; they are no more to thee than the dust of the earth, and to boast of them is to boast of that which hath no existence. The son of a captive, who hath risen to be a Bashaw of Three Tails, has reason to be proud, but the descendant of emperors, who is sunk into a wretched slave, ought to be ashamed to appeal to his ancestors. Go thy ways, and trouble me no more, or—" here he cast his eyes significantly on the naked scimitar lying at his side. Crispo retrograded from his presence, and departed in that unhappy state of mind in which a man has neither the philosophy to endure nor the courage to resent contempt.

"The Christian dog!" muttered Djezzar, as he retired—"Does he think I will quarrel with my physician, who might revenge himself by poisoning me with the first dose he administers?"

Matters were in this state, when a fellow who resided in the suburbs of the city, whose name was Policarpo, and who, besides being a thief and a robber, was suspected of being guilty of still more atrocious crimes, died of a malignant fever, and having neither money, effects nor friends, was buried without the usual fees to the papas, the bishop, the arch-treasurer, the archivist, and the Patriarch of Constantinople. Of course he was a fair subject for the Vroucolacas; and, accordingly, scarcely was he cold in the grave, when the citizens of Candia began to be disturbed at nights with various and unaccountable annoyances; appalling noises and unseemly visitations clearly indicating that the spectre demon was abroad. At first he merely amused himself by entering certain houses, tumbling around their goods and chattels, putting out the lights, and then pinching the inmates behind, black and blue, or raining such a shower of dry blows on their shoulders as was evidently supernatural. It was also affirmed that he dealt in terrible threats in case any one refused his request, whatever it might be, and had been heard to declare in the silence of midnight, in the ears of more than one person of good credit, that unless he was properly conciliated there should be neither rest nor safety in Candia.

Matters became so serious that a public meeting was called, at which Signor Crispo presided, and for which offence he was that very night visited by the Vroucolacas, and pinched and threatened almost out of his wits. Many papas, caloyers, and monks attended, and after long deliberation it was resolved to adopt the only mode ever known to be effectual in silencing these spectre demons, namely, that of disintering the body of Policarpo, extracting the heart, and consuming it by fire. This was accordingly performed with great ceremony, but wonderful to relate, the Vroucolacas, as if aggravated to new enormities by this rough treatment, became, if possible, ten times worse than before. The good people were, of course, frightened in like proportion, most especially as the person who performed this operation of extracting the heart solemnly declared that the interior of the body, though it had been interred ten days before, was as warm as that of a living person. Others affirmed the blood was most unnaturally red; and others again, that the body was at first perfectly flexible, and afterward became as hard and stiff as a mummy. People gathered together in crowds, shouting through the streets the name of Vroucolacas, and rending the air with a repetition of that musical, sonorous sound. But the obstinate demon only waxed more intractable and tormenting. It was the opinion of some of the papas that they had committed a great oversight in not burning the heart of Policarpo on the seashore, where there would have been plenty of room for the Vroucolacas to escape; but as there was no possibility of repeating the experiment, the truth or falsehood of this theory could not be fairly tested.

Every succeeding night increased the perplexity and dismay of the good people of the city. They met every morning to debate on the subject, and devise ways and means for quieting this obstinate demon, who equally resisted fire and water. Processions were made several nights in succession; they obliged the papas and caloyers to fast till they were almost starved to death; they ran about all day sprinkling the streets and houses with holy-water, washing the doors, and pouring it, as they said, down the throat of the Vroucolacas. They next proceeded to the grave of Policarpo, where they stuck naked swords into it, which they pulled out several times a day, and every time thrust them in still deeper. The failure of this last expedient having occasioned a sagacious caloyer to suggest that the handles of the swords being made in the form of the cross must needs prevent the demon, who of course stood in great awe of such an emblem, from budging an inch; they tried other weapons, but to no purpose—the Vroucolacas was incorrigible.

The consternation now became indescribable, for the demon grew every night more presumptuous and daring— increasing in his pranks with every expedient to keep him in order, while rumor invented a thousand new extravagancies. He took to ordering people to do this, that and the other thing, according to his own will and pleasure, and punished their neglect or disobedience by pinching or beating them soundly the very next night; he was accused of breaking down doors; ripping up the roofs of houses; knocking and chattering at windows in an unknown gibberish; tearing clothes, and emptying all the jars, bottles and wine tubs, for he was a most thirsty demon. In addition to all this, he discovered and blabbed so many secrets, and invented so many scandals, that he nearly set the whole community together by the ears.

What increased the terror and perplexities of the citizens, was the untoward circumstance of the papas not knowing the precise name of the evil spirit who had thus got possession of the body of Policarpo, nor what saint to invoke in this terrible predicament. Whole families began now to pack up their goods, and retreat to the neighboring isles of Syra, Tinos, Milos and Argentiera; and there was great reason to apprehend that if the Vroucolacas persisted in his persecutions, the whole city, if not the entire country, would be depopulated. The demon continued in the meantime to disseminate so many abominable slanders, that almost every family was at feud, and there was scarcely a good character left in the city, except that of Florentia, and the family of Dr. Constantachi, who, it was somewhat remarkable, continued entirely exempt from the annoyances of the demon.

But not so with the illustrious Signor Crispo Sanudo, who had, from the first appearance of the mysterious non-descript, come in for more than his full share of attention. Notwithstanding all the care he took to protect his premises, there being at that time, as at the present, neither locks nor bolts in Candia, the demon never failed in paying his nightly visits, and after diverting himself with a variety of malicious devices, such as putting out the lights, turning the furniture upside down, drinking his wine, and breaking his crockery, invariably concluded by giving him a hearty pinch, and uttering in an awful voice, "I will never cease until thou givest thy daughter Florentia to my particular friend Miquelachi, son to the great physician Constantachi." Signor Crispo continued, however, to hold out manfully, and swore he would do no such thing; whereupon his pinches were repeated with additions and improvements. Florentia, shut up in a remote part of the house, heard or saw nothing of all this, and when the signor detailed his grievances, would intimate to him that it was in all probability only a dream, arising from eating too many pomegranates for supper.

"Head of my ancestors!" would Crispo exclaim in a fury— "Do you think dreams could cover me thus with black and bloody bruises? I tell you that schismatic hound, Miquelachi, is in league with the Vroucolacas. But it won't do—I tell you it won't do. I'd rather be pinched to a jelly, and be deviled for a thousand years, than disgrace my illustrious ancestors—not forgetting Michael, the Stammerer—by calling that low-born slave my son."

"But, my father, is he not descended by the mother's side, from the Justiniani of Scios?" said Florentia meekly.

"The Justiniani! pooh, what are they compared with the Pascologii, the Comnenii, the Porphyrogenitii, and the Grand

Dukes of the Archipelago—not forgetting Michael, the Stammerer? I tell you, it won't do. I swear by their dust, their bones, and their immortal memory, that sooner than see you the wife of that Greek schismatic, I would consign you to the black eunuch of the seraglio." It should be premised that Crispo said this with a mental reservation, that Djezzar should not propose to him the alternative of the scimitar or the bowstring.

About this period it began to be whispered abroad, from some mysterious source, that all these public calamities were owing to the obstinacy of Signor Crispo, who refused to bestow his daughter on Miquelachi, son of Doctor Constantachi, notwithstanding the repeated instances of the Vroucolacas, who, for some secret reasons of his own, had set his heart on the match. A deputation of the oldest and most respectable citizens accordingly waited on Crispo, to remonstrate against his thus involving his native city in trouble and dismay by his obstinacy, entreating him to relent for the good of the community. But he scoffed at their solicitations, and repeated a hundred times—"It won't do—I tell you it won't do."

The deputation then determined to lay the whole affair before the Bashaw, who had just returned from fleecing his flock in the remote parts of his paschalic, just in time to receive their application. Djezzar forthwith commanded the attendance of Signor Crispo, his daughter and Miquelachi, omitting the Vroucolacas, who was the principal delinquent, for reasons best known to himself. In good time they appeared—Crispo pale with apprehension—Florentia shivering under her long white veil, and Miquelachi displaying the most perfect self-possession. The Bashaw was seated on his thread-bare cushion, his long pipe in his mouth, his scimitar naked by his side as usual, and attended by two janizaries, the silent executioners of his will and pleasure.

"Dog, and son of a dog," said Djezzar, with great gravity and severity. "What is this I hear? They tell me the good people of the city, not excepting the faithful, are grievously afflicted by the visitations of the Vroucolacas, as he is called in your heathen Greek jargon, to the great damage of their property, their rest at night, and their peace of mind by day, so that many have abandoned the island, and more are on the eve of going. It is moreover delivered to me, that the spectre demon—whom may the Prophet confound—has repeatedly declared that he will never cease tormenting the good people, until thou givest thy daughter, Florentia, to this young man, son to my learned physician, Dr. Constantachi, as his wife, and that thou dost obstinately refuse his reasonable request. Dog, and son of a dog, is it so?"

"I cannot deny it, your highness," faltered the signor.

"And why dost thou refuse?"

"He is not her equal in descent. My daughter is of the Pascologii, the Comnenii, and the Sanudos, while he is only the son of a physician."

"Bah!" exclaimed Djezzar impatiently—"Let me hear no more of this. Is not his father my physician, and has he not the life of the representative of the Prophet in his hands? Doth not this place him above thy dead ancestors, who could not preserve their own lives, much less those of others? And did I not once tell thee I am the son of a slave? Know, egregious fool, that there is but one man above another in this world, and that is the commander of the faithful, my master. All others are equal, and all his slaves. What other objections hast thou?"

"He is of the Greek, I of the Latin Church. He does not acknowledge the holy father at Rome as its head, but blasphemously bows to him they call the patriarch of Constantinople."

"By the beard of the Prophet, but this is a wonderful difference. Is there any God but God, any other head of the church but Mahomet? And is not the patriarch of Constantinople appointed by his representative, the grand signor, my master, solely in consideration of twelve hundred paras, presented by the scoundrel Greeks, for the pleasure of being plundered and excommunicated for their pains? What use then in differing about one point where all is wrong? Hast thou any other reasons to urge? Be quick, for I am very tired."

"I was about contracting my daughter to a descendant of the illustrious family of the Cornari, in Venice."

"Mashallah! what, the obstinate infidel dog, who defended this city four-and-twenty years against the arms of the commander of the faithful, and occasioned the loss of an hundred thousand of the true believers? Say no more. I will have none of that accursed breed propagated here. But enough. Dost thou consent to the demand of the Vroucolacas and the prayers of thy neighbors?"

"I cannot—my birth, my religion, and my honor, forbid."

The Bashaw made a sign to the janizaries, who seized Signor Crispo, and prepared that fatal bowstring, the very thought of which gives even a true Mussulman a touch of bronchitis. At this moment Florentia reached forward and cast herself at the feet of the Bashaw, beseeching him to spare the life of her father. In her agitation her veil had been cast aside, and she appeared in all the pride of beauty, become more exquisitely touching from the deep feelings of her heart.

"By the beard of the Prophet," exclaimed Djezzar—"a Houri—she is too beautiful for the arms of a Christian dog, and I must consider whether to make her my tenth wife, or elevate her to the celestial happiness of administering to the delights of the commander of the faithful."

Saying this, he seemed to reflect on the subject deeply, while Signor Crispo remained in the keeping of the janizaries, without once thinking of his illustrious ancestors; Miquelachi for the first time exhibited great agitation; and Florentia continued on her knees in agonizing despair.

"It is settled," at length said Djezzar, "I shall send her a present to the commander of the faithful, as a proof of my gratitude for his bounty. She is too beautiful even for a Bashaw of three tails, and shall depart tomorrow in the galley destined for Constantinople, as you Christian dogs call it. Away, fellows! and leave this Houri with me. I have said it."

Florentia sank to the ground, while Crispo remained mute as a statue, overpowered by a sense of his approaching fate, and the degradation preparing for his only child. Miquelachi, after hesitating a moment, came forward, and saluting Djezzar with profound respect, asked in a fine voice—

"May it please your highness, will this rid your faithful subjects of the visits of the Vroucolacas? It was for that we were called before you."

"Mashallah! I had forgot the demon entirely. But there is no help for it now, and he must play his part till he is either tired, or has drank up all the wine, when I suppose he will depart in peace."

"If your highness will recall the sentence against the daughter of Signor Crispo, I pledge my head to rid you of the Vroucolacas."

"Bah! what care I for that fool's head of thine? It is mine already whenever I choose to take it. Depart, I say, or I will make your shadow shorter by a head."

At this moment the venerable Doctor Constantachi made his appearance. He was the only man in the island the Bashaw either feared or respected. He stood in awe of his great skill, which had more than once been exercised on his own person, and could never divest himself of the idea that the doctor could as easily kill as cure him. For these reasons he always treated him with great courtesy and respect—partly from gratitude, partly from fear. The doctor came to plead the cause of Florentia, knowing how dear she was to his son, and the Bashaw was pleased to listen graciously to his suit, which involved in fact the only practicable mode of ridding the city of its diabolical persecutor, who had so frequently intimated the sole condition on which he would discontinue his visits.

"But if he should break his word," cried Djezzar; "these demons are slippery fellows, and fear neither the law nor the Prophet."

"May it please your highness, I—"

"But it does not please my highness that you should give any more pledges," said Djezzar, interrupting Miquelachi.

It is doubtless possible, notwithstanding the testimony of

all orthodox historians, poets and romance writers—by which latter we mean travelers—to the contrary, that a follower of Mahomet may, by way of miracle, possess some bowels of compassion, and occasionally, as it were, degenerate into an act of justice or humanity. Djezzar was cruel in conformity with the spirit of his religion and the maxims of his government, which held life cheap in comparison with the mild, merciful, and forgiving doctrines of Christianity. He also was guilty of violence and extortion toward those he governed; but here, too, he only acted in conformity to the universal custom of all the great and little dignitaries of the Ottoman Empire. He had bought his office at the price of eight hundred paras, and considered himself fairly entitled to extract at least three times that sum from the pockets of his subjects; more especially as he at the same time incurred the imminent risk of going the way of almost all Mussulman flesh in high station, and dying suddenly of a sore throat. On the whole, he was not a bad man for a Turk.

Djezzar had from the first decided on a compliance with the conditions demanded by the Vroucolacas, as a means of quieting the apprehensions of the people, and at the same time doing a good turn to his old friend the doctor, who had traveled a great deal and seen so many varieties of human faith, that so far from being a bigot, he might be said to be almost indifferent to all religions. He was exceedingly fond of his son, and anxious for his marriage with Florentia, because the young man declared it was indispensable to his happiness. It was with a view merely to operate on the personal fears and parental affection of Signor Crispo, that he had affected to proceed to such entreaties. Apparently, however, being moved by the arguments and entreaties of Dr. Constantachi, he addressed himself once more to Signor Crispo, and proposed as the last alternative either that he should give his daughter to Miquelachi, or lose her forever, and his life in the bargain.

While the father was hesitating, the young man suddenly threw himself at the feet of the Bashaw, exclaiming—

"Spare her and spare her father! I cannot consent to receive my happiness at such a price. I resign the dearest treasure of my life, provided you will spare that of Signor Sanudo, and permit his daughter to remain with him, to soothe his declining age."

"And what will the Vroucolacas say to that?" asked Djezzar. "He will rage ten times more than ever, and very likely attack me in my own castle. It will not do—either the consent or the bowstring. I perceive maiden thou art going to entreat me again. But spare your words—the consent or the bowstring."

Signor Crispo was observed to be greatly agitated. The truth is, though a vain and somewhat silly man, he was not altogether insensible to generous emotions. He was, therefore, not a little touched with the frank manly style in which Miquelachi had interfered in his behalf, as well as the disinterested sacrifice he had offered to make. There was, however, a still more powerful motive gradually acquiring greater force and energy, namely, fear of the bowstring, which, not being one of the faithful, he held in great abhorrence. After a succession of writhings and grimaces, and just as the Bashaw had given the signal to the janizaries, there bolted from the mouth of Signor Crispo, as if precipitated by some violent inward explosion, the following words—

"I consent—and may my illustrious ancestors, the Pascologlii, the Comnenii, the Porphyrogenitii, and the Sanudos—not forgetting Michael, the Stammerer—forgive me!"

"Mashallah!—by the beard of the Prophet," cried Djezzar, "but thou hast decided wisely for once, after being a fool all thy life; and as for thine ancestors, with the long names, depend upon it they won't trouble you about the matter. See that thou keepest thy word, and art kind to this young man, who must possess great merit since he is patronized by the Vroucolacas, and most especially to the beautiful Houri, thy daughter—or," here he cast a significant glance at the awful bowstring which caused Signor Crispo to tremble even to the soles of his slippers.

The Bashaw decreed that the marriage should take place on the spot, dispensing with all preliminary ceremonies, such as were practiced among the Christians of Candia. His word was law and gospel too, and the young lovers were forthwith married, to the satisfaction of all parties except Signor Crispo, who looked as if he had just lost all his illustrious ancestors. He continued discontented and sour for some time, but the fear of the Bashaw kept him from any overt act of unkindness; and when in the natural course of human events Florentia presented him with a grandson, he was in great perplexity as to the name he should bestow on him. At last he hit upon the happy expedient of calling the young stranger—who, by the way, had a vivid impression of a pomegranate on his left shoulder—Comnenius Pascologus Crispo Sanudo Miquelachi, with which he was quite delighted, seeing there were four to one in his favor.

The most remarkable circumstance, however, attending or rather succeeding this marriage, was, that the Vroucolacas kept his word like a demon of honor, and from that time ceased his nightly visits. When it was clearly demonstrated that he had departed, the people of the city began at first to doubt whether he had been there at all. Then they began to laugh at each other for believing it; and finally ended in laughing at themselves, perfectly unconscious that if the same thing were to happen again, they would be just as much frightened as before. Whether Miquelachi had any agency in the exploits of the Vroucolacas was never perfectly known. Florentia often bantered him on the subject, but he was too discreet a man to trust his wife with a secret of such consequence.